Jump For Joy was so special and beautiful that he hardly seemed real. . . .

"Chloe?"

Sharon's voice drifted into her ear. When Chloe finally tore her eyes away from Jump For Joy's head, she saw Sharon standing nearby, her hands on her hips, looking at her with one questioning eyebrow raised high. "Are you all right?" Sharon asked her.

Chloe still couldn't speak. She nodded once and fixed her gaze right back on the pony.

"Go ahead and pick up a trot," Sharon told her.

Trot? Suddenly Chloe was paralyzed. The word sounded like a foreign language to her.

"Chloe?" Sharon's voice came from behind her now. "Can you hear me?" Sharon asked. "I want you to trot."

Trot! Chloe willed her legs to press against the pony's sides. She couldn't tell if they had moved or not.

Trot! Trot! Chloe's mind was saying it, but her legs weren't moving. While Jump For Joy walked she felt safe. Trotting would change everything.

Trot! Her eyes were squinting as she tried to concentrate. If Jump For Joy trotted, he might canter. What if his canter was too fast? What if he decided to run, and she couldn't stop him? If he cantered, he might buck. What if he bucked very hard, higher than Bo Peep? What if she couldn't stop him from bucking and he hurt his leg again?

Chloe had to trot. Sharon had said so. *Trot,* Chloe mouthed, without a sound.

Books in the SHORT STIRRUP CLUB™ series (by Allison Estes)

Available from MINSTREL BOOKS

Friends to the Finish

Allison Estes

Published by POCKET BOOKS
New York   London   Toronto   Sydney   Tokyo   Singapore

This book is a work of fiction. Names, characters, places and incidents are products of the author's imagination or are used fictitiously. Any resemblance to actual events or locales or persons, living or dead, is entirely coincidental.

A MINSTREL PAPERBACK *Original*

A Minstrel Book Published by
POCKET BOOKS, a division of Simon & Schuster Inc.
1230 Avenue of the Americas, New York, NY 10020

ISBN: 0-671-00100-0

First Minstrel Books printing November 1996

10 9 8 7 6 5 4 3 2 1

SHORT STIRRUP CLUB is a trademark of Simon & Schuster Inc.

A MINSTREL BOOK and colophon are registered trademarks of Simon & Schuster Inc.

Front cover photo by Pat Hill Studio

Printed in the U.S.A.

To the Barn Rats at Claremont, young and old (Isa and Marika, Chloe and Jenny, Megan and Max, Margaux, Audrey, Marianne, Florence and Jackie, Greg and Barbara), and anyone, anywhere, who's ever loved horses and wished for a horse of his or her own.

"Short Stirrup" is a division in horse shows, open to riders age twelve and under. Additional requirements may vary from show to show.

Friends to the Finish

1

A RAY OF SUNLIGHT CREPT AROUND THE EDGE OF A white eyelet curtain and beamed upon the blond girl sleeping in the twin bed. Chloe Goodman slowly opened her deep green eyes and looked around her bedroom. She knew by the color of the late August light seeping through the curtains that it was still very early in the morning. She didn't have to get up yet; school didn't start for another week. Chloe closed her eyes again and tried to recall the dream she'd been having. It had been so pleasant. . . . She remembered a field of purple flowers and the feeling of cantering on a horse. . . . She let her mind wander back along the path toward sleep again. Soon she saw the field of flowers and smiled as her white pony, Jump For Joy, whinnied and came trotting through the meadow toward her—

"Oh!" Chloe's eyes snapped open. The beautiful image vanished as she sat upright in bed. She had just remembered: this was the day the veterinarian was coming to check her pony, Jump For Joy, to see if he was finally ready to be ridden again!

Anxious to get to the stable where she kept her pony, Chloe sprang out of bed and hurried to pull on a pair of cutoff overalls over the T-shirt she had slept in. She brushed her teeth and caught her pale blond hair in a hasty ponytail, then tiptoed into her mother's room. Her three-year-old brother, Michael, lay sleeping in his crib, surrounded by an army of ragged stuffed animals. Chloe paused to look at him. He had really outgrown the crib, but her mother couldn't afford to buy another bed. Besides, with only two small bedrooms in the house, there was no place to put an extra bed.

Chloe's parents were divorced. Her dad, who lived in Arkansas, came to see his son and daughter only once in a while. Kathryn Goodman, Chloe's mom, waited tables at the Beacon Diner. She was studying to get her realtor's license so that she wouldn't have to work long hours at the diner to earn a living. She had promised Chloe more than once that when she was selling houses instead of hamburgers, they would all be better off.

"Mama?" Chloe said softly.

2

Her mother opened her eyes. "Hmm?" she said sleepily. She had worked very late the night before.

"I'm going over to Mamaw's. She'll drive me to the barn, okay?" Chloe whispered.

"Take Michael," Kathryn Goodman murmured, closing her eyes again.

Chloe made a face. *"Ma-ma,"* she pleaded, "he's still sleeping. I'm in a hurry because the vet is coming to check Jump For Joy's—"

Her mother cut her off. "Chloe, please. Take Michael to Mamaw's. I didn't get home 'til nearly two in the morning, and I've just got to get some sleep."

Chloe crossed her arms. She took care of her brother often, and mostly she didn't mind, but today she wanted to get to Thistle Ridge Farm early. The vet was coming at eight o'clock, and she wanted to be there when he arrived. Her grandmother, who lived just up the street, would drive her to the stables, but if she had to get Michael up and ready, it would take extra time.

She stared wordlessly at her mother. Then she remembered how hard her mom worked, now that her father didn't live with them. She sighed and went to wake up her brother. "Thank you," she heard her mother say from the bed.

Michael was already awake. "Ch'oe," he said happily when he saw his big sister. He stood up and held out his arms for her to take him.

"Hey, big boy," Chloe said, lifting him out of the

crib. "Want to go to Mamaw's?" As quickly as she could, Chloe dressed her brother. He was just learning to wear underpants instead of diapers. "Want to go to the potty?" she encouraged him.

"No!" Michael said firmly. "I don't have to."

"Okay," Chloe said, carrying him into the kitchen. She gave him a banana to eat while she went out to the carport to feed her dog and cat.

"Sorry, Missy," she said to the long-haired gray cat winding itself around her ankles. "There's no more cat food." The bag of dry dog food was mostly full. Struggling to tilt the heavy bag enough to pour some food into both dishes, she managed to spill half of it. "Shoot!" she said, staring with dismay at the pile of dog food on the cement floor. Before Chloe could stop her, Jenny, her black Lab, leaped enthusiastically into the pile and began to eat, scattering dog food all over the carport.

"Oh, no," Chloe groaned. "At this rate I'm never going to get to the barn." When she had swept up most of the mess, she made sure the animals had water, then went to get her brother.

"Michael?" she called. She had left him at the kitchen table, but his chair with the booster seat was empty. Banana was smeared all over the table. Chloe went to look for the little boy and found him in the bathroom, his pants soaking wet.

"I go potty," he said proudly.

"Oh, Michael," Chloe groaned. "That's very good,

but next time take off your britches first." She went to find dry pants for him, but the dresser drawer was empty. From a pile of dirty clothes by the washer she dug out the cleanest pair of shorts she could find and put them on him. Then she had to wipe up the banana mess. Finally, she took Michael by the hand and led him up the street to her grandmother's house.

"Mamaw," Chloe's grandmother, often took care of Chloe and her brother when their mother was working. When Chloe came in through the patio door, Mamaw was sitting at the kitchen table drinking instant coffee. "How're my grandbabies this mornin'?" Mamaw said.

"Fine," Chloe said, giving her grandmother a hug and a kiss.

"Michael, give Mamaw some sugar," Mamaw demanded. The little boy ran to kiss his grandmother. "My goodness, who dressed this child?" she said, smoothing Michael's messy blond hair as she frowned at his clothes. His shorts, an old pair of Chloe's, were two sizes too big and covered with faded flowers. "He looks like a ragamuffin."

"Waganuffin," Michael agreed.

Chloe felt embarrassed as she looked at her brother. "He wet his britches, and these were the cleanest ones I could find. I didn't have time to brush his hair," she explained hastily, then said, "Mamaw, can you please drive me over to the barn

5

right away? Dr. Pepper's coming to check Jump For Joy's leg today to see if he's ready to be ridden again. I *have* to be there." Chloe glanced at the clock. It was already past seven-thirty.

"Did you have breakfast?" Mamaw asked.

Chloe shook her head. "I didn't have time. Can we go, please?"

"You need to eat something," Mamaw insisted. "There are biscuits on the stove."

Chloe wasn't hungry. To please her grandmother she took two biscuits and wrapped them in a napkin, saying, "I'll take them with me. Can we go now? Please, Mamaw?"

"All right, all right," Mamaw said, getting up from the table. "Now, where's my purse?" she said, looking around for it. "I declare, I'd lose my head if it wasn't screwed on."

Growing frustrated, Chloe watched while her grandmother poked around the kitchen and living room, searching for her purse. Finally Chloe began to look for the bag herself. She spotted it on the kitchen counter. "Here it is," she said, bringing the black vinyl bag to her grandmother.

"I'll declare," Mamaw laughed. "If it'd been a snake, it would have bitten me!"

"Can we go now, Mamaw?" Chloe asked very sweetly. Inside she was crawling with impatience. She glanced at the clock again—quarter to eight.

All she wanted to do was get to the barn by eight o'clock, but it was beginning to seem impossible.

Somehow Chloe managed to get her grandmother and brother out of the house and into the car. The air conditioner was blasting full force in Mamaw's green Pontiac as they drove slowly to the stables, but the car was still unbearably hot. Chloe shifted impatiently on the vinyl seat, searching for a cooler spot. She adjusted the air-conditioning vent so that it blew directly on her face, wishing for the thousandth time that she lived close enough to the stables to walk or ride her bike, like her best friend, Megan.

Chloe had met Megan Morrison and her twin brother, Max, earlier that summer, when they had moved to Hickoryville, Tennessee, from Connecticut. Before meeting them, Chloe had been having the worst year of her whole life. She had been taking riding lessons for several months, and her father had promised to buy her a pony. Most of the other kids who rode at Thistle Ridge had their own horses and ponies. Then her father lost his job. Her parents separated, and right before Christmas her father moved to Arkansas to look for work.

Everything had changed after that. Chloe's whole life was different in ways she didn't like at all. She loved both her parents and couldn't see why they wanted to be apart, especially when it seemed to make things so much harder for all of them. Her parents were angry at each other, so she couldn't talk to them about how she felt. And she missed her father. Since he'd left, her mother had to work very hard to support her and her brother. Chloe tried to help her mom with the chores as much as she could, but sometimes she wished things would just go back to the way they had been. She felt she had lost something important, but she didn't know how to begin to get it back.

What Chloe loved most of all was riding horses. When her dad had moved out, Chloe had been afraid she was going to lose that, too. Kathryn Goodman had managed to keep paying for Chloe's riding lessons, but Chloe had known without asking that buying a pony was out of the question. She had been feeling very sad and lonely.

Then Megan and Max had come to Thistle Ridge Farm. Max had a horse, and Megan had her own pony, Pixie, a little dapple-gray mare. Chloe and Megan had quickly become best friends. Chloe remembered how nervous she had been before her first horse show. She hadn't had the proper clothes to wear in the show and had been scared to death that the school pony she was riding, Bo Peep, would buck her off. Megan had taught Chloe how to sit a buck, so that she wouldn't be afraid of falling off. Together with her brother and another friend, Keith Hill, Megan had come up with show

8

clothes for Chloe. And best of all, because of Megan, Chloe had gotten a pony of her own.

Jump For Joy, Chloe's pony, had once belonged to Amanda Sloane. Amanda's parents were very wealthy and bought her whatever she wanted. Jump For Joy was a fancy, expensive show pony who had carried his young rider around safely and beautifully. But Amanda was spoiled and careless. In the horse show she had ridden recklessly, causing her pony to slip and severely injure his leg. Everyone had thought his leg might be broken, but the vet had examined it and told the Sloanes that the injury was a pulled suspensory ligament. Jump For Joy would be out of work for many weeks while the torn ligament healed.

To everyone's shock and horror, Amanda's father, Gerald Sloane, had refused to pay for the pony's care. He told Amanda he would buy her a new pony. Even worse, he had ordered the vet to give Jump For Joy an injection to end his life.

Chloe remembered how heartbroken she had been when she heard that the beautiful pony would have to be put down. She had always loved Jump For Joy and wished that somehow he could belong to her. She brushed him whenever Amanda would let her and spent all her spare time stroking him and talking to him.

Chloe always felt that it was a mistake that Jump For Joy belonged to Amanda. She couldn't help feeling that Amanda didn't deserve to have him because she treated him so carelessly. "You should have belonged to me," she had often whispered to the pony. "We were meant to be together." And the pony seemed to feel the same way. His ears always pricked forward whenever he saw Chloe coming to groom him. It was plain to see that Jump For Joy loved Chloe as much as a pony could love a person.

If it hadn't been for Megan, Chloe remembered, Jump For Joy would be gone. Megan had persuaded the Sloanes to give the pony to Chloe. And Sharon Wyndham, the owner of Thistle Ridge Farm, had agreed to let Chloe do barn chores to pay for Jump For Joy's board and care.

"Every cloud has silver lining," Chloe's grandmother was fond of saying. Chloe understood what that meant. Some dark clouds had come into her life, but in the middle of them she had found her best friend, Megan, and her beloved pony, Jump For Joy. As long as she had Megan and Jump For Joy, Chloe felt she could handle anything.

Chloe's grandmother drove very slowly. The eight-mile drive seemed to take forever. Finally, Chloe saw the familiar green-and-gold sign with the horse jumping over a thistle, which hung from a cedar post at the entrance to Thistle Ridge Farm. The car crept up the long driveway, lined on either side with pecan trees and white-fenced paddocks where horses were turned out to play and graze. Chloe curled her fingers around the door handle and listened to the gravel crunching under the tires as they approached the big white barn at the top of the driveway. Stretched around her, as far as she could see, were acres of green hilly pastures decorated with ponds and stands of shade trees. Feeling surrounded by horses, Chloe sighed happily.

" 'Bye, Mamaw, thanks for driving me," Chloe said, when they had at last pulled up in front of the stables. She gave her grandmother a quick kiss and jumped out of the car.

"Good-bye, darlin'," her grandmother said. "Do you need to be picked up?"

"No, thanks," Chloe said. "I can get a ride home with Megan."

" 'Bye-bye, Ch'oe," Michael said wistfully from the backseat. He put his thumb in his mouth.

" 'Bye-bye, Michael," Chloe said, blowing him a kiss. "Don't be sad. You and Mamaw will have fun today. I love you!" she said cheerfully as she closed the door.

"Lo' you," Michael said around his thumb.

Chloe waved at him as the car headed back down the driveway. She stooped to pat Fancy, one of the barn cats, who was winding herself in a figure eight around Chloe's ankles. She fed Fancy the two biscuits she had brought from her grandmother's house and stuffed the napkin into her pocket. Then, with a little skip, she hurried into the barn.

2

Chloe remembered to walk when she was inside the barn. It was a rule, just like at a swimming pool. Except, Chloe knew, at a swimming pool the rule was so you wouldn't slip and fall. At Thistle Ridge you weren't supposed to run because you might spook a horse.

When she had first learned to ride horses, Chloe wondered how such a huge animal could be frightened so easily. Horses spooked at all kinds of things that didn't really seem threatening. Balloons, baby strollers, bicycles, certain sounds, and people running or making sudden moves could all panic a horse. But Chloe read every book she could find about horses. She had learned from her reading that horses have a very strong "flight" instinct; at the least sign of something unusual, a horse's first instinct is to run away.

Sometimes, when she felt overwhelmed by her chores at home and at the barn, Chloe imagined herself turning into a horse and running swiftly away. She would graze in a green pasture all day and lie down with the herd at night in the cool grass. She wouldn't have any more dishes to wash, or homework to do, or stalls to muck out. She wouldn't have to worry about her parents fighting all the time. Life would be simple and free. She could almost feel her long tail swishing away at the flies and taste the grass as she tore up juicy mouthfuls and swallowed them down.

A low, hopeful whinny interrupted her daydream. Chloe smiled as she recognized her pony's voice. She saw him standing with his face pressed up against the bars surrounding the top of his stall, his ears pricked forward with anticipation. Chloe felt herself growing happier by the second as she approached her pony's stall.

"Hi, pony," she said in the special tone of voice she always used to speak to him.

Jump For Joy snickered in reply. He shifted his weight, as if he were looking for some way to walk out of the stall, then stood still again, gazing intently at Chloe over the wall of the stall. His white face, with its gray muzzle and large, intelligent brown eyes, looked so beautiful to Chloe that she wanted to cry.

She undid the latch on the door and went into the pony's stall. He stepped toward Chloe and began nuzzling her with his soft nose. She put her arms around his neck and kissed the perfect white arch of it over and over. Then she stroked his nose as Jump For Joy began to lick her arm. Chloe giggled at the feel of his warm, wet tongue. "I'm so lucky to have you," she murmured.

"Not as lucky as that pony is to have you, Chloe."

Chloe looked up to see a familiar friendly face topped by a red St. Louis Cardinals baseball cap. It was Pepper Jordan, the veterinarian. "Hey, Dr. Pepper," Chloe said.

He nodded in reply. Peering into the stall, he said, "That pony sure has taken a shine to you, hasn't he?"

Chloe nodded. "He loves me," she said. "And I love him."

Dr. Pepper chuckled. "There's not much doubt about that. Bring him out here, will you, and let's see if he's fit to ride." The vet stood aside while Chloe got a lead line and halter and fastened them around the pony's head.

I wish Megan would hurry up and get here, Chloe thought nervously. She had counted on her best friend being with her while Dr. Pepper examined the pony. Since Megan was more experienced around horses, Chloe always felt reassured just having her nearby. The day before they had planned on meeting by the stall early. *So where is she?* Chloe wondered. She led her pony slowly out of the stall, watching his left front leg anxiously to see if he was limping. He seemed to be walking normally.

"Just hold him there while I get set up," Dr. Pepper said. Along with his medical bag, he had brought a yellow case with switches and meters on it. Chloe knew by now that it was the ultrasound equipment. The vet hooked the yellow box up to a moniter and turned it on. The tiny television screen began to glow with blue light. He took a stretchy, curly cord and hooked it up to a handheld scanner.

"Hey, Pepper," Sharon Wyndham said.

When Chloe glanced up and saw Sharon strolling down the aisle toward them, she automatically stood up straighter. Sharon had that effect on people; she was always so professional and correct, it tended to rub off on others. But Chloe had learned that Sharon's heart was as good as the gold medal she had won riding in the Olympics. Like most of the kids at Thistle Ridge Farm, Chloe would have done anything to please Sharon.

"Hey, Sharon," Chloe said.

"Good morning, Chloe," Sharon said with a smile.

Not for the first time Chloe wondered how

Sharon always managed to look so clean and proper when she worked all day in a barn. Though it was still early, Chloe knew that Sharon had already exercised a couple of horses and maybe even mucked out a stall or two. But her sleek riding breeches were spotless. So was her bright blue polo shirt, which matched her eyes. Her blond hair was gathered smoothly into a ponytail, and her lipstick looked as if she had just put it on. Chloe couldn't see even a drop of sweat on Sharon's face, though outside the temperature was already close to ninety degrees.

Chloe looked at her own clothes. The T-shirt she wore was wrinkled from having been slept in and already had a smear of dirt across it. Her cutoff overalls were filthy; she had worn them the day before. Her tennis shoes, inherited from an older cousin, were battered and scuffed. She could feel the wisps of hair that had escaped from her ponytail sticking to her sweaty face. She wiped her face on her shirtsleeve and concentrated on feeling cool.

"Sharon, have you seen Megan?" Chloe asked.

Sharon thought for a moment. "No, not this morning," she said. "Amanda's here, though. Why don't you ask her if she's seen Megan?"

Chloe nodded at Sharon, but she knew she wasn't going to ask Amanda Sloane where Megan was. Amanda had always acted stuck-up and rude to Chloe, no matter how friendly Chloe tried to be.

And ever since Chloe had become owner of Amanda's old pony, Chloe found it even harder to talk to the girl.

"How does he look, Pepper?" Sharon asked, indicating Chloe's pony.

"Well, we're about to find out. The last ultrasound pictures we took were pretty good. That torn ligament ought to be healed by now, but we'll know for sure in just a minute."

Chloe remembered how she'd spent the long summer months taking care of Jump For Joy, waiting for his leg to heal. The pony had been injured at the horse show in late spring. For several weeks he had to stand in his stall. Dr. Pepper had warned her that the pony wasn't supposed to walk at *all*. Chloe had felt so sorry for Jump For Joy, just standing in his stall for weeks and weeks. When the period of stall rest was finally over, Chloe had been glad to start hand-walking her pony. For a month she led him around the barn twice a day for fifteen minutes, his legs bandaged with polo wraps to support the damaged ligament. It wasn't so simple to wrap a horse's legs just right, but Chloe had finally learned to do it almost as well as Allie Tatum, the head groom. When the ultrasound scans began to show that the ligament was healing nicely, Dr. Pepper told Chloe that Jump For Joy could be turned out in a paddock to roam by himself. The first few times he was turned out, he had to be tranquilized to keep him calm so he wouldn't run around in his excitement and reinjure his leg. Chloe remembered that at first he had limped whenever he trotted, but lately he had been looking more and more like the beautiful mover he had been before his injury. She wanted more than anything for her pony's leg to be completely healed so that she could ride him at last.

As Dr. Pepper started the ultrasound scan, Chloe's stomach felt like it was full of squirrels. She crossed the fingers of both hands and hoped for the best. She watched the vet squirt some blueish jelly from a tube onto the handheld scanner and on the pony's leg.

"Dr. Pepper, I've been meaning to ask you. What is that goop you put on his leg?" Chloe asked curiously.

The doctor explained that the jelly would help conduct the sound waves as they were transmitted, bounced off the muscles and ligaments inside the pony's leg, and returned to the scanner. The vet put the scanner on the pony's leg and began to move it slowly up and down, searching for the site of the injury. Chloe, Sharon, and the vet all watched intently as a picture of the bone and tissue on the inside of Jump For Joy's leg appeared on the monitor.

"There it is," Dr. Pepper muttered, holding the scanner in place. He pointed to a spot on the screen. "That's where the tear was. See how it's all closed up?"

"I see it," Chloe said, fascinated by the detailed picture. "I remember how the tear looked. It's all gone now, isn't it?" Chloe asked hopefully.

"It looks good, real good." Dr. Pepper nodded, still staring at the screen. He abruptly put down the scanner and switched off the machine. "That was the worst torn suspensory ligament I'd ever seen, and it's healed better than any I've ever seen," he said, sounding satisfied. "Chloe, you've taken good care of this pony. Let's take him outside, and let me see you jog him once before I pronounce him fit to ride."

Leading the pony, Chloe followed Sharon and Dr. Pepper out the back door to a flat, grassy area behind the barn. There was an old section of wooden fence there, grown over with honeysuckle. Chloe remembered with a shudder that it was the very spot where Jump For Joy's life had nearly ended— when his former owners, the Sloanes, had ordered him put down. Chloe stroked her pony's neck lovingly and mentally thanked her best friend, Megan, for the thousandth time. Megan's quick thinking had saved Jump For Joy.

Where was Megan? She had promised to meet Chloe, and it wasn't like her not to show up. All through the summer Megan had helped Chloe with Jump For Joy. She had taught Chloe to wrap his legs and had spent hours beside Chloe while she hand-walked the pony. Megan knew this was the day Jump For Joy might be officially healed. Why wasn't she here?

"Okay, let's see him jog," Dr. Pepper said.

For the moment, Chloe forgot about Megan. She began to lead Jump For Joy in a circle at the walk. Then she clucked at him, encouraging him to trot. He obediently picked up a quick trot. Chloe jogged along beside him while Sharon and Dr. Pepper watched for anything uneven in the pony's strides.

When she had jogged him in both directions, Dr. Pepper told Chloe she could walk. "I guess that's all I need to see," he said.

"Well?" Chloe asked anxiously. "Is he . . . is he okay?"

Dr. Pepper smiled reassuringly at Chloe. His blue eyes twinkled in his tan face as he said, "That pony's sound as a dollar, Miss Chloe. You can start riding him as soon as you're ready."

"Oh!" Chloe squealed with delight. "Hooray!" She gave a little skip. "Did you hear that, pony?" she said to Jump For Joy. "Dr. Pepper says you're all better now. Aren't you glad?"

As if he could actually understand her words, the pony nodded his head up and down. Both adults laughed.

"If I didn't know better, I'd swear that pony understood what you just said, Chloe," Dr. Pepper said, amused.

"Of course he did. He understands everything I say to him. He's very smart," Chloe said proudly. "Aren't you, pony?"

Again, Jump For Joy nodded his head. "See?" Chloe said. She knew that horses weren't *really* supposed to be able to understand human speech. But sometimes it was tempting to believe it. After all, young horses were often trained to obey voice commands such as "halt" and "canter." If they could understand single words, Chloe reasoned, it wouldn't be that amazing for horses to understand a few words put together, would it?

"Well, if he could talk, I guess he'd be thanking you for taking such good care of him," Dr. Pepper said.

"When are you going to ride him, Chloe?" Sharon asked.

"Oh, as soon as I can!" Chloe exclaimed.

"Well, let me know when you're ready to get on him, so I can watch you. He may be a little fresh the first few times," Sharon cautioned.

"Okay," Chloe said. She was impressed that Sharon was going to take the time to watch her ride. Besides running Thistle Ridge Farm, and riding her own horses, Quasar and Cuckabur, Sharon trained other people's horses for them. Sharon and Quasar had won a gold medal for the

United States Equestrian Team at the Olympic games that year. And she was already preparing to qualify Cuckabur for the show jumping team at the next Olympic games.

Sharon also taught private or semiprivate riding lessons, but she charged more for her time than the other instructors at Thistle Ridge. Plenty of kids and adults trained with Sharon, including Megan and Max. Even Keith Hill, Max's best friend, took lessons from Sharon. But Chloe's mom couldn't afford private lessons. Chloe took a group class for one hour every week. She loved Leigh, her teacher, and had learned a lot in the class, but she often wished she could train with Sharon, too. Chloe usually watched Megan and Max's jumping lesson with Sharon. And while she watched, she always imagined herself in the lesson, too, riding with perfect form as she and her beautiful little white pony jumped gracefully around the arena.

When Dr. Pepper left with Sharon to look at another horse, Chloe led Jump For Joy back into the barn. Though she was delighted that he was well again, she felt disappointed that Megan wasn't there to share her excitement with her. The barn formed a T-shape, with the second aisle branching off exactly halfway down the main aisle. As she passed the second aisle, Chloe peered down it to see if she could see Megan. She thought she saw Max and Keith there and was about to call out to them when Keith's big sister, Haley, started up the aisle leading her thoroughbred mare, Cinnamon.

"Can I get by?" Haley said politely, if a little impatiently.

"Hey, Haley," Chloe said with a smile. She thought Haley was so pretty, with her short, dark hair. Haley was fourteen and the best rider of all the older boys and girls at the barn. Chloe had heard that Haley was going to try to qualify for the MacClay Equitation Finals at the National Horse Show.

Haley and Cinnamon went by her, and Chloe continued down the main aisle. She decided to give Jump For Joy an especially good grooming so he would be extra clean and shiny when she rode him for the first time. She hooked up the cross-ties to either side of Jump For Joy's halter. Then she took out her grooming kit and went to work.

With a hoof pick Chloe started by cleaning off the dirt that had caked up on the bottoms of the pony's feet. Starting with the right front, and being careful not to dig at the sensitive "frog" in the middle of the hoof, she began to pick out the foot. When she had removed every speck of dirt with the brush end of the hoof pick, she blew on the bottom of the foot, just to be sure it was totally clean. Then she moved to the right hind. She sometimes felt a little leery of picking up a horse's hind foot. She knew that even a very good horse *might* kick some-times, like Bo Peep.

Bo Peep was the school pony Chloe had been riding while Jump For Joy was lame. Whenever Chloe tried to pick out her hind feet, Bo Peep would jerk her foot away after only a few seconds. Allie, the head groom, had explained that Bo Peep had "string halt," a condition in her hind legs that made it hard for her to bend them. The jerking motion made Chloe a little nervous. Chloe had never been kicked, though she had seen Bo Peep kick out at other horses who came too close to her. Chloe was very sure she didn't want to risk getting kicked herself.

When she slid her fingers down the tendon at the back of Jump For Joy's hind leg, he raised his foot right up and held it there patiently while Chloe picked out the hoof. When she moved to do his left hind, he lifted it up before she even touched it. He did the same with his left front.

"You're such a good boy," Chloe said with relief. Cleaning Jump For Joy's feet was easy compared to cleaning Bo Peep's. Chloe blew the last bit of dirt off the pony's left front foot and set it down gently, remembering that that had been the in-jured leg.

Next, she took a rubber currycomb, slipped her hand under the strap on the back, and went to work currying the pony. She started with the left side of his neck, scrubbing in a circular motion to lift all the loose dirt and hair. She worked her way back to his rump on that side, then started again with the right side of his neck.

"You're going to be the cleanest pony in the whole barn," she said, knocking the currycomb against the wall to get the dirt out of it. When she had curried him everywhere except for his head and the bony parts of his legs, she knocked the currycomb against the wall again and put it away.

Taking a stiff, natural bristle brush, she began to brush Jump For Joy. She worked with firm, deep strokes, going from front to back so she wouldn't brush dirt onto the part she had already cleaned. Chloe remembered the first grooming lesson Allie Tatum had given her. Allie had shown her how to give the brush a little upward flip at the end of each stroke to lift the loose dirt away from the horse's coat. Chloe used the stiff brush all over the pony's body and his legs, everywhere except his face.

"Don't worry," she said as Jump For Joy flinched at the first feel of the stiff bristles on his sensitive belly. "I won't brush too hard." She waited until he was standing quietly again, then very gently finished brushing his belly. Chloe remembered how she had hated to see Amanda rake the brush over the pony's tender underside, never noticing that it made him uncomfortable. Amanda didn't seem to enjoy taking care of horses; she did it carelessly, if she did it at all, mostly relying on the grooms to clean her horse for her. Chloe loved working around horses on the ground, and had learned more about their personalities from grooming them than she had from actually riding them. Allie had taught her that it was important to become very familiar with her pony's body. That way, if he ever had a swollen leg or a strange bump, she'd notice it right away. Chloe knew every inch of Jump For Joy, from his dainty gray muzzle to the tip of his long, gleaming tail. Many times she had petted him with her eyes closed, memorizing every contour of his sleek, muscular frame. She often wondered why anybody who loved riding horses wouldn't love grooming them just as much.

When she had been over Jump For Joy's body with a soft "dandy" brush, she carefully brushed his face. With a large-toothed metal comb, she picked the tangles out of his tail until it hung straight and shining. She was careful to stand to the side of his hindquarters, out of kicking range, while she worked. The pony's mane and forelock were pulled thin and short, so they didn't need much combing. Last, Chloe took a "rub rag," an old, soft, clean towel, and wiped him down with it. The rag acted like a dust magnet, picking up whatever stray hairs and dirt were left on the animal.

Then she shook out the rub rag and stood still,

eyeing the pony for any dirty spot she might have missed. He stood politely, looking back at his young mistress, his little ears pricked forward, waiting for whatever was coming next. His white coat couldn't have been cleaner if he had just been bathed. Chloe couldn't help smiling. "You are *so cute*," she said happily. She went to him and kissed his soft nose. "I can't believe you're really mine," she whispered to him as she gazed at his beautiful face.

Chloe stood transfixed, admiring her pony and thanking her lucky stars for him. When she was little, she had believed in fairy godmothers and had envisioned one for herself, dressed in a filmy blue gown. Now she was too old to believe in fairies, but she wondered wistfully if there might be some sort of Spirit of Goodness who watched over and protected innocent children and animals. She imagined a mysterious winged creature, like an angel, barely visible, who hovered in the air somewhere nearby. Had there been a spirit there the day Jump For Joy had nearly died? Had the spirit chosen to save Jump For Joy and see that he was given to Chloe? She was so entranced in her dream that she didn't notice the shape of a large white horse looming in the doorway at the end of the barn. But when the horse's hooves clattered loudly on the concrete floor, Chloe nearly jumped out of her skin.

"Loose horse!" a groom yelled.

"It's Prince Charming again!" another groom shouted.

Chloe recognized Amanda Sloane's new horse, Prince Charming, headed in her direction. He was always getting loose somehow.

"Heads up, heads up!" someone warned.

Chloe realized in a panic that the horse was thundering down the aisle, gaining speed. He was headed straight for her and Jump For Joy!

3

WITH THE SOUND OF HOOFBEATS POUNDING BEHIND HER, Chloe dashed to her pony's side and started to unclip the cross-ties from his halter so she could move him out of the way. She was afraid Prince Charming would run right through the cross-ties and Jump For Joy would be pulled to the floor. But the clip on the cross-tie was stiff and refused to release. Prince Charming came barreling toward them. Chloe gave up on the clip and began waving her arms frantically, hoping to stop the horse. Prince saw the cross-tie and skidded to a stop, sparks flying as his shoes scraped the concrete. He came to a halt just a split second before he would have run right into the cross-tie. The big horse hesitated only a second. He lowered his head and ducked under the cross-tie, then galloped the rest of the way to his stall, hooves sliding and sparks flying.

Startled by the commotion, Jump For Joy swung his hindquarters to the side, away from the loose horse. He bumped into Chloe hard, and she reeled backward and fell against the tack trunk. Jump For Joy's metal shoes slipped on the concrete, and he scrabbled frantically, trying to regain his footing. For a few awful seconds, Chloe was sure Jump For Joy was going to fall down right on top of her. The pony planted his feet at last and stood quivering, his eyes white-rimmed with fear.

Prince Charming trotted through the open door of his stall, letting out a satisfied snort. He turned himself around and stuck his head out of the stall, swinging it from side to side as he looked expectantly from one end of the barn to the other. He reminded Chloe of someone searching for a waiter in a restaurant.

Chloe sat on the floor where she had fallen, trying to decide if she was hurt. She had landed hard, but for a second she only felt numb. Then searing pain shot through her lower back, where she had banged it against the tack trunk. Tears welled up in her eyes as she bit her lip and tried not to let them fall.

"Oh, my gosh, Chloe! What happened?"

Chloe recognized her best friend's voice and saw

through her tears the blurry shape of Megan hurrying toward her. She raised her arm and wiped her eyes with her shirtsleeve. Her elbow was badly scraped where she had landed on it.

Megan knelt by Chloe's side. Tucking a lock of her wavy brown hair behind her ear, she peered into Chloe's face. Megan's brown eyes were full of concern as she spoke. "Are you okay?" she asked anxiously.

Chloe nodded. She wasn't sure she could speak without crying. She slowly started to get up. Vicious pain shot through her back, but she gritted her teeth and managed to get to her feet.

"What on earth happened here?"

Chloe glanced up and saw Allie Tatum striding toward them. Allie was tall and sturdy, with wide-set blue-green eyes and lots of thick, wavy brown hair. Her large, strong hands were battered and scarred from working around horses and barns all day. Allie knew more about how to handle horses than anybody Chloe had ever seen, even Sharon. She treated all the horses at Thistle Ridge as if they were her children; when Allie said "the kids," she was talking about the horses. Allie wasn't afraid of any horse, no matter how big or badly behaved. Even the most stubborn, ill-tempered horses quickly responded to her by doing whatever she asked of them. Chloe wished she were as brave and sure of herself around horses as Allie was.

Allie pushed Prince Charming's head back into his stall and slid the door closed. Then she came to stand beside Chloe. "What happened?" she demanded again.

"I was bringing Prince Charming up from turnout, and—" Megan started to explain.

"Why were *you* bringin' him up?" Allie interrupted. "Why wasn't Amanda bringin' her *own* horse up?"

At that moment Chloe noticed Amanda Sloane standing silently nearby. Amanda, as usual, was dressed as if she had just appeared on the cover of *Horse and Pony* magazine. She wore spotless, expensive jodhpurs and a pale green show shirt with a choker collar. The satin ribbons at the ends of her blond braids matched the shirt exactly.

"Well?" Allie said, looking from Amanda to Megan. "I'm waiting."

"Amanda asked me to lead him up for her," Megan said.

"Megan asked me if she could lead him," Amanda said at the same time.

Amanda wasn't very confident about handling Prince Charming. She would squeal and drop the reins or the lead line if the horse even looked at her funny. So Prince Charming was always getting loose. Usually he would run toward the pasture when he escaped, unless he was hungry. Then he'd

32

head for the nearest open stall, hoping to find grain in the manger.

Chloe could see that Amanda was trying to blame Megan for letting Prince get loose this time. But Chloe knew how much Megan admired Amanda's horse. Megan had even let Amanda ride her beloved pony, Pixie, at a show a few weeks before so that Megan could ride Prince Charming. Chloe was pretty sure that Megan had been glad to lead Prince Charming because she liked the horse, and that Amanda had been just as glad not to have to handle him.

"Amanda," Allie said sternly, "if you can't handle your horse by yourself, come get me or one of the other grooms to bring him up for you—not Megan."

Chloe saw Megan give Amanda a look that said, "Hah. You're not getting me in trouble."

Then Allie continued, "And, Megan, you tend to your own pony. I saw you go off and leave her alone on cross-ties again. Didn't you learn your lesson about that?" Chloe knew Allie was talking about the time Pixie had spooked on the cross-ties and fallen. Pixie's legs had gotten stuck against a wall, and she had narrowly escaped being badly injured.

"But, Allie, Max was right there!" Megan protested. "He was keeping an eye on her for me."

Allie went on lecturing Megan. "Max was busy

33

with his own horse. How's one boy supposed to look after two animals? I put Pixie back in her stall, and I'd better not find her on cross-ties again unless you're right by her side." Allie stood with her hands on her hips, waiting for Megan to say something.

"Okay, Allie," Megan said sheepishly. Then she turned to Chloe and said earnestly, "Chloe, I'm really sorry about this morning. I got to the stables early, so I went to watch Prince in turnout while I waited for you to get here. I only meant to stay down there for a minute. Then I got so interested in watching him, I completely forgot what time it was. I meant to be there when Dr. Pepper came, really I did."

Chloe could hardly believe that Megan had been at the barn all morning. The whole time Dr. Pepper had been checking Jump For Joy, Megan had been watching Amanda's horse run around in turnout! Feeling a mixture of surprise and hurt, Chloe wondered how Megan could have forgotten what an important day it was for her and Jump For Joy.

"Now suppose you tell me—how did that horse get loose *this* time?" Allie asked Megan.

"I was leading him out the paddock gate," Megan explained. "He was just walking along. Suddenly he started snorting and stomping his feet and sort of jumping around. I tried to hold him, but he was dragging me, so I had to let go. Then he ran up

34

the hill toward the barn. I'm really sorry," she said sincerely. "I never saw a horse act like that. What do you think was the matter with him?" Megan asked.

"Hmm," Allie mused. "Sounds like maybe a bee stung him."

"Oh, do you think that's what it was?" Megan asked.

"Probably," Allie replied. Then she noticed the huge scrape on Chloe's elbow, where she had fallen on it. "My gosh, Chloe, what happened to you?" she asked.

Chloe's back still felt like fire blazed through it every time she took a breath. But she had almost gotten used to it. Her voice was only a little quavery when she spoke. "Jump For Joy shied away from Prince when he ran by. He accidentally bumped into me, and I fell against the tack trunk." Chloe gestured with her uninjured arm.

"Well, you need to wash that elbow and put somethin' on it. Come to the office with me, and we'll get you fixed up," Allie said. "Are you hurt anywhere else?"

"It's mostly my back," Chloe said.

Allie gently lifted the bottom of Chloe's shirt and looked at her lower back where it had grazed the corner of the metal trunk. She whistled softly.

"That must hurt," Megan said sympathetically.

Chloe nodded, wincing at a sudden stab of pain.

Her back throbbed, but her feelings were hurt even more. She was so disappointed in Megan that she couldn't even look at her. She stroked Jump For Joy's neck and kept her eyes on his legs.

Suddenly Chloe noticed a bright red splotch on the barn floor near Jump For Joy's left front foot. Forgetting all about her own pain, she bent to look more closely at her pony. There was a wound on the back of his left front ankle, just above the hoof, and it was dripping blood.

"Oh, no!" Chloe wailed. "Allie, Allie, come quick! Jump For Joy is hurt. Look! Look right there on the back of his ankle." She pointed to the injury.

Allie squatted near the pony's leg and examined the back of his ankle. "Looks like he stepped on himself and cut it," she said. "It must've happened when Prince ran by him." She straightened up. "Well, the first thing to do is take him over to the wash stall and rinse it with cold water, so I can see just how deep it is."

"Oh, poor pony," Chloe moaned. "And it's his bad leg! Oh, I hope he's not going to be lame again." Chloe led Jump For Joy to one of the two wash stalls. She deliberately didn't look at Megan, who was walking beside her.

Having nothing better to do, Amanda trailed behind them. Chloe watched anxiously as Allie hosed the pony's leg with cold water, revealing an inch-long gash at the back of his ankle.

"Is it very bad, Allie?" Chloe asked. "Is he going to need stitches?"

Allie bent and peered at the cut, then stood up, keeping the hose flowing on it. "No," she said, "That ain't too bad—just a little nick, that's all. Looks like he clipped himself with his back foot. Just keep the hose turned on it till it stops bleeding. He'll be fine," she reassured Chloe.

"Thank goodness," Chloe said, feeling relieved.

"Here," Allie said, holding out a blue jar of antibiotic ointment. "When it stops bleeding, dry it off and put some of this on it."

"Okay," Chloe said, taking the jar from Allie.

"And don't forget about your arm and your back." Allie pointed to the scrape on Chloe's arm, which was now smeared with dirt and dried blood. "That needs to be cleaned and covered with a bandage."

"I'll help her take care of it, Allie," Megan said quickly.

Allie went back to the main barn, leaving the three girls in the wash stall with the pony. Chloe watched the blood seep out of the cut on Jump For Joy's leg and wash away in the flow from the hose. She still felt hurt that Megan hadn't been there when Dr. Pepper came to examine Jump For Joy. And she couldn't help feeling a tiny bit angry at both Amanda and Megan for letting Prince Charming get loose.

"It looks like it's stopped bleeding," Megan suggested after a few long, silent minutes.

Chloe turned off the water and blotted the cut with some paper towels. She opened the jar of ointment and carefully dabbed the gooey yellow medicine on the wound. Then she put the medicine and the paper towels back on their shelf. She started to coil up the hose, but Megan took it from her.

"I'll put the hose away," Megan said quickly.

"Thanks," Chloe said.

"What did Dr. Pepper say?" Megan asked, as she coiled the hose around the hook on the wall. "Did he do the ultrasound?"

Chloe nodded. "He said the tear in the ligament is all healed up now. And when I jogged Jump For Joy, he didn't limp at all."

"That's great!" Megan said, sounding genuinely glad for her friend.

Chloe began to feel her anger dissolve. It was hard to stay mad at Megan; whenever she did something wrong, she always worked twice as hard to make up for it. "He says I can ride him whenever I want," Chloe said quietly. A shy smile crept into one corner of her mouth and spread across her face.

"Oh, Chloe, aren't you glad? I know how long you've been waiting to ride him!" Megan said excitedly.

"When are you going to get on him?" Amanda

spoke up. She had been standing in the furthest corner of the wash stall the whole time, trying not to let any water splash on her shiny paddock boots.

Chloe hesitated. "Tomorrow, I guess," she said. "I'd better give him a day to rest his ankle."

"Allie said his ankle is just fine." Amanda stepped forward, seeing that the hose was turned off, and folded her arms. "Why don't you get on him today?" she demanded.

"Yeah, Chloe," Megan joined in. "Aren't you dying to ride him? If I were you, I'd get on him right this second!"

Chloe looked at Amanda, who gazed coolly at her with her pale blue eyes. She looked at Megan, who had begun to chatter away about all the things Chloe was going to be able to do, now that she had her own pony to ride. But Chloe wasn't really paying attention to Megan. She was thinking about riding Jump For Joy.

Chloe remembered the first time she'd ever seen Jump For Joy. She'd been riding Bella, one of the old school horses used for beginner lessons, and was struggling to keep the horse trotting while she learned to post. 'Up-down-up-down, one-two-one-two,' her teacher chanted, while Chloe bumped up and down in the saddle and steered Bella in a wobbly circle around the arena. She remembered how impossible it had seemed and how tired and frustrated she'd felt.

Then Jump For Joy had trotted by her with Amanda posting smoothly on his back. Chloe stared at the beautiful white pony, dazzled by his gleaming coat and his darling little face. At the time, Chloe had thought that Amanda must be a very advanced rider because she looked so polished and elegant on the pony's back. While Chloe was busy admiring her and her pony, Amanda steered Jump For Joy right in front of Chloe's horse, cutting her off. Bella stopped to avoid bumping into the pony. Chloe lurched forward, bumping her nose on Bella's neck. Her teacher had hurried over to see if she was all right while Chloe watched Amanda canter off without a backward glance.

But when her nose had quit smarting, Chloe went right back to working on her posting trot. Jump For Joy had inspired her. She envisioned herself riding the way Amanda had on her beautiful pony. Chloe stuck her heels down, sat up tall and straight, and made her legs squeeze firmly every time she posted down. Bella perked up and trotted in a lively, even circle around the arena while Chloe posted smoothly up and down, never missing a beat.

After that lesson, Chloe had made it a point to watch Amanda ride Jump For Joy whenever she could. She tried being extra friendly to Amanda, who was just as snobby as ever. But Chloe was fascinated with Jump For Joy and determined to find a way to be near him. She learned that Amanda was lazy about cleaning her tack, so Chloe offered to clean the saddle and bridle for her if Amanda would let her groom and pet Jump For Joy. Soon Amanda would look for Chloe whenever she was done riding and simply hand over the pony to Chloe to put away.

"How can you let her order you around like that?" Megan had once asked Chloe. But Chloe never cared how Amanda spoke to her. She simply loved being near Jump For Joy, though she had never actually ridden him.

Amanda and Megan were both still watching her, waiting for an answer to their questions. The two girls couldn't understand Chloe's hesitation.

Suddenly, Chloe's stomach was full of butterflies. She remembered that Amanda had been riding since she was six years old, and Megan even longer. Chloe had been riding only a little more than a year.

All the time Jump For Joy had belonged to Amanda, Chloe had wished that she could ride him. During those long weeks when his leg was healing, she had dreamed of what it would be like to finally get on her own pony. But now Chloe had only one thought, and it wouldn't go away. It filled her with dread, and it was this: *What if I'm not good enough to ride him?*

4

MEGAN AND AMANDA LOOKED AT CHLOE CURIOUSLY, still wondering why she didn't want to get right on her pony as soon as she could.

"I think I'd better wash off this scrape on my elbow first," Chloe said. She started to unclip the cross-ties so she could lead Jump For Joy back to his stall.

"I'll take Jump For Joy back to his stall," Amanda said quickly.

Surprised at Amanda's offer, Chloe stared at her quizzically. It was completely unlike Amanda to be helpful.

"I'll take him for you," Amanda insisted.

"Okay," Chloe said, wondering what had come over Amanda. "Thanks."

Megan went into the bathroom with Chloe and helped her wash off the scrapes on her elbow and back with soap and water. Chloe winced and sucked air into the sides of her mouth as the water touched her back. "That stings," she gasped.

"Sorry," Megan said, dabbing gently at the wound with a wet paper towel.

"What does it look like?" Chloe asked. She half turned, trying to see her back in the mirror above the sink.

"You have a big gouge from hitting the corner of the trunk. It's not really bleeding, but I can see a bruise starting," Megan told her. "You could use a Band-Aid back here, too," she added.

"Megan, why do you think Amanda offered to take Jump For Joy for me?" Chloe asked.

"I don't know," Megan admitted. "It's pretty weird isn't it?"

"I've never seen her help anybody before," Chloe said. "Even when Jump For Joy was her pony, she always let me take care of him."

"Must be temporary insanity," Megan suggested. "Maybe Mrs. Sloane will get it, too. Next thing you know, they'll be inviting us over for a tea party! 'Mandy honey, pass your little friends the angel food cake. And sit up straight,'" Megan said in a southern drawl. She tilted her head and made a gesture with one hand that was a perfect imitation of Mrs. Sloane.

43

Chloe laughed out loud. Amanda's mother didn't seem to like anyone very much, least of all Megan. Megan could be outspoken, and her behavior wasn't always "proper" enough for Mrs. Sloane.

Still giggling, the two girls went to the barn office. Allie put antiseptic ointment and bandages on Chloe's back and elbow. When she had finished, Allie said, "There. How's that?"

"If feels much better," Chloe said. "Thanks, Allie."

"Come on, I'll help you get Jump For Joy tacked up," Megan said.

"Just be sure you find Sharon and have her there when you get on him," Allie cautioned her. "That pony hasn't had anybody on his back in nearly three months. There's no tellin' how he'll behave."

"We will," Chloe promised.

"Oh, he'll be good, Allie," Megan said. "He loves Chloe. He'll be glad to have her riding him. Come on, Chloe. I'll help you get him ready. I'm so excited that you're finally going to ride him, aren't you?" Megan was practically skipping as they went out the door of the office.

"Oh, yeah," Chloe said. "I can hardly wait!" She made her voice sound cheerful, but inside she felt the butterflies start again. What if she couldn't handle Jump For Joy? What if he acted wild because he hadn't had a rider on his back in so long? What if he bucked her off, or tried to run away with her? Chloe had been riding Bo Peep all summer. She

44

knew the little mare so well now that she could make her do anything. Jump For Joy might be completely different. If she rode him the same way she rode Bo Peep, would he pay attention to her?

"Megan?" Chloe said.

"Yeah?"

"Do you think that's really true what you said to Allie, about how Jump For Joy will behave for me because he loves me?"

Megan looked curiously at her friend. "Of course it's true. He knows you better than anybody. He'll be good."

"But how do you know?" Chloe asked.

"You know how Pixie is, right?" Megan said.

Chloe nodded. Megan's pony, Pixie, was quick and spirited. She sometimes spooked at sudden movement or sounds. But most of the time when Megan was riding her, she behaved perfectly.

"Remember how Pixie acted when Amanda rode her in the horse show?" Megan reminded her. Chloe recalled that Pixie had been startled by a quail that flew up from the grass at the edge of the ring. She had bolted around the ring with Amanda, who couldn't stop her. "Pixie would never have behaved like that with me on her," Megan said. "She knows me too well. Except for that one time when she spooked at the deer," she added, remembering when Pixie had run with her all the way from the back pasture to the main barn, jumping a few large fences on the way.

"But you've been riding since you were really young!" Chloe protested.

"So has Amanda," Megan countered.

"But you're used to Pixie. I've never ridden Jump For Joy," Chloe finally admitted. "What if I can't do it?"

"You can do it," Megan said confidently. "If Amanda could ride him, *anybody* could."

Chloe hoped Megan was right. The two girls found Amanda waiting with Jump For Joy at his stall. Chloe picked up a brush. The pony was clean as could be, but she began brushing him energetically anyway, pretending to have found a dirty spot on his rump.

"Where's your saddle?" Amanda asked.

Chloe's brushing became slow and deliberate. "I don't have a saddle," she said without looking at Amanda. "But Sharon said I could borrow Bo Peep's saddle."

"I'll get it," Megan offered, going to the tack room. In a minute she was back, saying, "It's not there. I guess someone's riding Bo Peep in a lesson."

"I guess I'll have to wait until they're done then," Chloe said with relief. "I have to use Bo Peep's bridle, too." At least she could put off the ride. Maybe

46

she wouldn't feel so nervous if she had a little while longer to think about it.

"Oh!" Megan said. "What am I thinking? You can use my tack. Jump For Joy and Pixie are about the same size."

"Thanks," Chloe said doubtfully, as Megan went back to the tack room and got her saddle and bridle. Chloe laid the fluffy white saddle pad on Jump For Joy's back. She carefully set the saddle on top of it. Going around to the right, "off," side of the pony, she buckled the girth to the first and third billets. Then she went back around to the "near" left side and carefully tightened the girth. She was careful to pull smoothly on the billets to tighten the girth gradually. Allie had shown her how yanking on them would pinch the soft skin under a horse's belly. That was why some horses snapped with their teeth when they felt the girth being tightened; they had learned to fear being pinched.

When Chloe had finished putting on the saddle, Megan handed her Pixie's bridle. Chloe had memorized all the parts of the bridle from a book about bits and bridles long before she ever learned to put one on a horse. She cleaned tack to help pay Jump For Joy's board and could take apart a bridle and put it together again faster than anybody except Allie.

Chloe unclipped the cross-ties and put the reins over Jump For Joy's head. Then she guided the bit into his mouth with her left hand, while with her right hand she pulled the crownpiece up and over the pony's left ear. When the bit was in place behind his back teeth, on the "bars" of his mouth, she gently pulled his other ear between the crownpiece and the browband. Once the browband was settled across his forehead, she pulled his white forelock out from under it. She buckled the throatlatch and checked to be sure she could fit four fingers sideways between it and the pony's cheek. Allie had explained to her that when a horse lowered his head, he could put a foot through a throatlatch that was too loose. Chloe had never seen that happen, and she didn't want to. And, she knew, if the throatlatch was too tight, it could choke the horse. Then she checked to be sure the noseband was exactly two finger-widths below the pony's cheekbones before she buckled it under his chin, not too tight and not too loose.

"Does this look like it fits him okay?" she asked Megan. She knew if the bit was too high in a horse's mouth, it would feel uncomfortable. If it was too low, she had learned, a horse could put his tongue over the bit or take it in his teeth. Then the rider wouldn't be able to communicate with the horse.

Megan took a look at the corners of Jump For Joy's mouth, where the bit rested. There were two wrinkles in the dark skin by the pony's mouth, just above the bit. "Yep," Megan said. "Exactly two wrinkles. We don't even have to adjust the cheek-pieces. Jump For Joy and Pixie have the same size head!"

"I guess we're all ready then," Chloe said.

"Not quite," Megan said. She pointed to Chloe's bare legs and her battered tennis shoes. "You can't ride in shorts and sneakers."

"Oops," Chloe said. "I forgot."

"You can borrow my chaps if you want," Megan offered, unzipping them and handing them to Chloe.

Chloe pulled a pair of scuffed brown paddock boots from her trunk and sat down on it to put them on. Then she zipped Megan's chaps on over her shorts. "Now I'm ready," she said, trying to sound confident. But her fingers shook as she fastened her safety helmet under her chin.

"I'll go find Sharon," Megan said. "We'll meet you down by the ring."

"Okay." Chloe waited until Megan was out of sight. She glanced around to be sure nobody was listening. Then she spoke to Jump For Joy.

"Pony, I have something to tell you," Chloe began in a hushed voice. "In a little bit, I'm going to ride you." She regarded the pony, who stood patiently, as if waiting for her to continue. "I'm going to get on your back and walk you around a little—just a walk!" she added hastily. "I want you to promise

49

me you won't buck me off or make me look like a bad rider in front of Sharon and Megan, okay? Just be your normal self, and don't forget that you've been hurt for a long time. Now that you're well again, you've got to be careful," she warned. Then she looked sternly at him. "Promise?"

Somehow the pony chose that moment to swing his head up and down, just as if he were nodding "yes."

Chloe said in a satisfied tone, "Good. Then I guess we're ready to go down to the ring." She took Jump For Joy's reins and led him out the back door. It was still early morning, but the hot sun was already trying to outdo the cool breeze that blew across the ridges all day. Thistle Ridge farm sprawled over a hundred seventy acres of rolling hills and areas of flat bottomland. The main barn was built on one of the highest hills, with the rings and paddocks just below it. Chloe started down the sloping path to the big outdoor ring, with Amanda following behind.

She passed the two buildings that housed the indoor rings, big and small. There was a little round ring used for longeing horses who needed to be worked down before they were ridden. Chloe had often seen Allie or Sharon standing in the center of that ring holding one end of the longe line, while a frisky horse, attached by his bridle to the other end of the longe, trotted or cantered around.

Beyond the big outdoor ring was the dressage ring, marked by letters at different points and surrounded by a looping chain fence. A woman trotted around on a big, pretty bay horse in that ring. Chloe recognized the rider; it was Mrs. Sloane. Chloe walked by quickly with her head down, hoping that Mrs. Sloane wouldn't notice her with Jump For Joy and come over to watch. Mrs. Sloane made everybody uncomfortable, especially Chloe.

Next to the dressage ring was a wide, flat, grassy field with several natural-looking jumps in it. That was the hunter ring. And there was another slightly smaller ring with no jumps in it at all. That was the small outdoor ring, where Chloe had had her first lessons. Her instructor, Leigh, was there now, teaching a private lesson to a boy riding Bo Peep.

Chloe led Jump For Joy into the smallest ring and waited for Megan and Sharon. Amanda climbed up on the fence rail and sat staring at Jump For Joy and Chloe, who wondered what Amanda was up to.

"Do you have a lesson today?" Chloe asked Amanda.

"Yes," Amanda answered. "I have a private jumping lesson with Sharon. I'm going to ride in the Charity Classic, you know," Amanda said smugly.

"Oh, that's nice," Chloe said. She had heard of the Charity Classic, one of the biggest horse shows in the area. It was an "A-rated" show that attracted

51

riders from all over the country. And, Chloe knew, some of the money raised at the show went to children's hospitals and other charities. The entry fees for some of the events were seventy-five or even a hundred dollars.

"I'm getting a new riding jacket and boots just for that show," Amanda said. "And Harry Hall jodhpurs. Mama says they're the very best."

"Oh, they are," Chloe agreed, though she had never heard of Harry Hall.

"Sharon says there might be nearly a hundred entries in the Short Stirrup division alone," Amanda remarked.

"A hundred!" Chloe exclaimed. "How can a judge remember who was the best out of so many entries?"

Amanda shrugged. "I suppose it's obvious. Some people have it, and some people don't."

"I guess," Chloe said.

"I rode him in it last year, you know," Amanda said, pointing at Jump For Joy.

Chloe tried to imagine what it would feel like to be all dressed up in the finest new riding clothes, trotting Jump For Joy around a huge arena with ninety-nine other children. She could picture how fancy Jump For Joy would look, with his mane done up in tiny perfect braids, his snowy coat shining. He belonged in that kind of a show. But she couldn't even begin to imagine herself riding in such a distinguished crowd.

"We got two third-place ribbons and a second-place in the pony hunters last year out of seventy-nine entries," Amanda gloated.

"Really?" Chloe said politely. "That's great."

"Mama says I'd win the pony hunter division this year if I was still riding Jump For Joy," Amanda told her. "She says it's a shame *you'll* never be able to show him to his full potential. But it takes talent and money. Mama says it's too bad you don't have either one," Amanda finished airily.

Chloe felt her face flush with anger and embarrassment. She knew that Jump For Joy had had a long and successful show career before the Sloanes had bought him for Amanda. And it was true Chloe would never be able to enter anything more than small local shows; her mom simply could never afford to pay the expensive entry fees at the big A-rated shows, never mind the other expenses of showing. But it was mean of Amanda to act like she was such a wonderful rider compared to Chloe. She had seen Amanda ride enough to know that it was Jump For Joy who made Amanda look like such a good rider. The pony was gentle and honest and patient, besides being a beautiful mover and jumper. That was why Amanda had done so well in shows, Chloe knew. Jump For Joy had cost the Sloanes twenty thousand dollars, and as far as

Chloe was concerned, he was worth it, every bit. She never doubted that she was very lucky to have such a pony.

She was trying to think of something to say to Amanda when she caught sight of Sharon and Megan coming down the path. Sharon's Jack Russell terrier, Earl, trotted along at her heels. Megan's brother, Max, and Keith Hill, his best friend, were right behind Sharon and Megan. Chloe was relieved that she didn't have to be alone with Amanda anymore.

The group entered the ring. Megan stood by the gate, waiting for Earl, who had stopped to pee on a clump of bitterweed.

"Earl!" Sharon called. "Come on!"

The little dog scampered through the gate, and Megan closed it behind him.

"Hey, Chloe, you wouldn't actually get on Jump For Joy without the rest of the Short Stirrup Club, would you?" Max asked her. Though Max and Megan were twins, they looked nothing alike. Max was taller and lankier than his sister, with light hair and eyes.

"Yeah, we'd hate to miss this," Keith said. Keith's father was Mexican, and his mother Native American. Keith had the tan skin and dark hair and eyes of his southwestern ancestors.

"Well, where have you guys been?" Chloe asked.

"We went on a trail ride this morning," Max said.

"We just got back," Keith added.

"It's a good thing we didn't go around the lake after all," Max said to Keith. "We're just in time to see Chloe finally get to ride Jump For Joy."

"All right, Miss Chloe," Sharon said smiling. "Let's get you up on this pony."

"Wait a second," Megan said. "Come on, guys." She stuck out her hand, and Keith, Max, and Chloe stacked their own hands on top.

"Short Stirrup Club!" the four kids cheered.

Out of the corner of her eyes, Chloe saw Amanda look away. Megan, Max, Keith, and Chloe called themselves the Short Stirrup Club because they were best friends and because they all rode in the Short Stirrup division in horse shows. Chloe sometimes felt bad that Amanda wasn't included, but at that moment she was glad. Amanda had really hurt her feelings. Chloe didn't really want an audience, but she was pleased that Megan and the boys had come down to watch her ride. It was better than having Amanda sitting there staring at her.

"Chloe, just remember," Sharon cautioned her, "Jump For Joy hasn't had a rider on his back in almost three months. He's had plenty of turnout, but be ready in case he decides to toss a buck, okay?"

"Okay," Chloe said. Inside she felt completely terrified. What if he bucked her off? Or worse, what if he somehow hurt his leg again?

"Are you ready?" Sharon asked her.

Chloe nodded yes, even though she wasn't ready at all. But she couldn't back down, not with so many people watching. "Can you give me a leg up?" she asked Sharon.

"Sure."

Chloe put the reins over Jump For Joy's head and around his neck. She walked to the pony's off side and pulled down the stirrup. Then she went to the other side and pulled down the near stirrup. Taking the reins in her left hand, she put the same hand on the crest of the pony's neck. She put her right hand near the pommel at the front of the saddle. She bent her left knee and turned to look at Sharon. "On three?" she asked.

"On three," Sharon agreed, taking Chloe's left leg in her hands.

Chloe faced the saddle again and took a deep breath. Bending her right leg slightly, she prepared herself to make a little jump when Sharon boosted her. Chloe's heart was thumping so loudly, she wondered if the others could hear it. She grasped Jump For Joy's mane in her left hand, tightly so they wouldn't see how her fingers were trembling. She swallowed hard and tried to work up some spit, because her mouth was so dry she could hardly speak.

"One," Chloe managed to croak. "Two," she said, bouncing a little on her right leg. "Three," she finally said. At the same time she jumped off her right leg and pushed up with her arms as Sharon gave her a boost. She swung her right leg over the pony's back and settled lightly into the saddle. Her feet found the stirrups and her fingers found the reins, and suddenly, in spite of how scared she was, Chloe felt as happy as she had ever been in all the twelve years of her life. She was finally sitting on her very own pony!

5

SHARON HELD ON TO THE REINS, WAITING TO SEE WHAT Jump For Joy would do when he first felt the weight of a rider after his long vacation. The pony just stood quietly. His large, brown eyes seemed to say, *What are you holding on to me for? I'm not going to do anything.* After a moment, Sharon let go.

Chloe dimly noticed the sound of applause and realized that Megan, Max, and Keith were all sitting on the fence, clapping and cheering for her. Only Amanda was silent.

"You can ask him to walk, Chloe," Sharon suggested.

Feeling numb, Chloe looked at Sharon and saw that she was smiling encouragingly. Chloe had to look at her hands to see if she was holding the reins correctly—she couldn't feel a thing. She looked at her feet and saw that the stirrup length was fine.

"Go ahead," Sharon encouraged.

Chloe wasn't sure if her legs would actually obey, but she willed her calves to press against the pony's sides. They must have done so, because Jump For Joy moved forward and started to walk around the arena. Chloe felt the four beats of his lively walk and heard the soft thump and scratch of his hooves as he stepped through the sandy footing. As her pony moved his head in time with the walk, she felt the gentle tug on her hands and remembered to let her elbows follow the motion. She knew she was supposed to look ahead with her eyes, but she was captivated by the sight of her pony's dainty ears pointing forward beyond the curve of his gleaming white neck. A bit of a breeze lifted sections of his feathery mane, which seemed to sparkle in the sunlight. Chloe remembered the fairy-angel she had imagined, wondering again if there could be such a thing. But she couldn't tear her eyes off her pony to look above her. Jump For Joy was so special and beautiful to Chloe that he hardly seemed real. At that moment she had the feeling that if she changed anything at all, if she even breathed differently, he might disappear, leaving her sitting in the sand on a lonely saddle, her empty hands poised where the reins had been.

"Chloe?"

Sharon's voice drifted into her ear. She sounded far away, but Chloe had walked almost all the way around the arena and back to her. When Chloe finally tore her eyes away from Jump For Joy's head, she saw Sharon standing nearby, her hands on her hips, looking at her with one questioning eyebrow raised high. "Are you all right?" Sharon asked her.

Chloe still couldn't speak. She nodded once and fixed her gaze back on the pony. Jump For Joy hadn't disappeared, but she looked him over from head to tail, just to be sure.

"Go ahead and pick up a trot," Sharon told her.

Trot? Suddenly Chloe was paralyzed. The word sounded like a foreign language to her.

"Chloe?" Sharon's voice came from behind her now, because Chloe had walked past her. "Can you hear me?" Sharon said in a stronger voice. "I want you to trot."

Trot! Chloe willed her legs to press against the pony's sides. She still didn't know if they had moved or not. Jump For Joy's head came up a little, and he cocked an ear back as if he were waiting for Chloe to tell him something.

"What's the matter with her? Can't she even make a horse trot?" A familiar nasal southern drawl reached Chloe's ears. It was Mrs. Sloane, who had come over from the dressage ring to watch. Chloe's head was frozen, but her eyes stole to the side and took in the sight of Mrs. Sloane near the in gate, sitting on Manfred, her big dressage horse.

Trot! Trot! Chloe's mind was saying it, but her legs weren't moving. While Jump For Joy walked, she felt safe. Trotting would change everything. What if his trot was bouncy? What if her hands pulled on his mouth by accident? She would look terrible. She would look as if she didn't deserve to have such a nice pony.

Trot! Her eyes were squinting as she tried to concentrate. If Jump For Joy trotted, he might canter. What if his canter was too fast? What if he decided to run, and she couldn't stop him? If he cantered, he might buck. What if he bucked very hard, higher than Bo Peep? What if she couldn't stop him from bucking and he hurt his leg again?

"What on earth is she doing, just sitting there?" The breeze carried Mrs. Sloane's disapproving words across the arena.

Chloe had to trot. Sharon had said so. *Trot,* Chloe mouthed, without a sound. Jump For Joy flicked both ears backward. He was trying to help her. Suddenly she realized why her legs wouldn't move. Her whole body was locked into a big ball of tension. She took a deep breath, in and out, and suddenly felt her hands and feet again. "Trot," she said out loud, and this time she felt her legs pressing against his sides.

Jump For Joy put his ears forward again and made a smooth transition from the walk to the quick two beats of the trot. Chloe automatically began to post, rising up and down slightly with the rhythm of the trot. She willed her hands to keep still, but in a few seconds, she realized she didn't have to. Jump For Joy's trot was springy but smooth as silk, the easiest kind of trot to keep up with. A moment before, she hadn't been aware that her heart was even beating. Now she felt it thumping boldy in her chest, and the beats seemed to be perfectly in time with the rhythm of her posting. Chloe knew she would remember the feel of this trot for the rest of her life. At the same time, she knew Jump For Joy wouldn't ever bolt, or even try to buck her off. A huge smile broke over her face. In the thirty seconds it took to trot back to the side of the ring where Sharon stood, she had memorized the feel of her pony. She hadn't cantered, but she knew what it would feel like; she realized she had always known. Now she couldn't imagine why she had ever dreaded riding him. She and Jump For Joy were meant for each other. He was familiar now and always would be. From that moment on, climbing onto his back would be the same as coming home.

Chloe squeezed the reins gently in her fingers, signaling Jump For Joy to walk, then halt. He responded instantly. Letting the reins get a little longer to reward him, she patted his neck lovingly. She glanced at the kids sitting on the fence and saw her friends smiling proudly. That gave her the courage to look Mrs. Sloane right in the eye. Mrs. Sloane sniffed and began to fuss with her reins. Then Chloe turned to Sharon and waited to see what she would say.

"You. Look. Great." Sharon gave Chloe's thigh an affectionate pat with each word. "How does it feel to be riding your own pony?"

Chloe couldn't stop smiling. "It feels wonderful!" she said happily. A minute before, she couldn't speak at all. Now the words tumbled out. "He has the best trot! It's so smooth, but it's kind of big, much bigger than Bo Peep's trot. I bet his canter is so nice. I can't wait to feel it. When do you think he'll be ready to canter, Sharon?"

"Well, you need to work up to it gradually," Sharon explained. "Today I would just walk him for another fifteen minutes or so. Then tomorrow you can do a little more trotting. Every day you increase the amount of work slightly, to give his muscles a chance to build up again. I'd say by the end of the week you could try some cantering."

"Hooray!" Chloe said. "I can hardly wait!"

Megan, Max, and Keith all jumped down from the fence and crowded around her. A second later, even Amanda came over to stand near them.

"Chloe, you look like you've been riding him all

your life," Megan said, patting Jump For Joy on the neck.

"Yeah, I can't wait to see you take him in a horse show," Max said. "You're going to clean up the blue ribbons!"

"Uh-oh," Keith said. "It looks like we're going to have to find another division to ride in. The competition's going to be too stiff in Short Stirrup, with Chloe riding Jump For Joy," he joked.

"Oh, no," Chloe said worriedly. "Please don't. You're my best friends. I would never even have made it through my first show if it hadn't been for y'all. I don't want to be in any horse show if you're not there," she said, looking at each one of them.

"He's just kidding, Chloe," Max told her. "Don't worry. Keith's got to keep showing in Short Stirrup until he learns to jump at least two feet!"

For a while, Sharon had been trying to get Keith to try jumping a little higher. She'd told him he was ready, and that when he jumped higher jumps, the littler jumps would seem easier. But Keith just wasn't interested in jumping more than eighteen inches, the height of a crossrail.

"I'm still just ten years old," Keith quipped. "That gives me at least two more seasons of showing in Short Stirrup."

"And I'm showing in Short Stirrup until I win a championship ribbon," Megan said determinedly. "So don't worry, Chloe—when you start taking

Jump For Joy to horse shows, the Short Stirrup Club will be with you all the way!"

"Sharon," Chloe said. "I just thought of something. Will Jump For Joy ever be able to jump again?"

All the children were silent, waiting to hear what Sharon's answer would be.

Sharon frowned as she studied the pony's legs. "Well, Dr. Jordan seemed to think that the tear in his suspensory ligament has healed completely." She looked up at Chloe and went on. "As long as we build up his strength gradually and keep the ligament supported with polo wraps, there's no reason why he shouldn't be able to jump again."

"Yes!" Megan grabbed air with her fist and pulled it toward her in a gesture of triumph. "I knew it. Chloe, you and Jump For Joy are going to be the best pony-and-rider team around."

Earl barked with excitement, as if he, too, were glad for Chloe. Sharon and the children shared a good laugh over the little dog's enthusiasm.

Only Mrs. Sloane and Amanda weren't laughing. "Hmmph!" Mrs. Sloane said, perched on Manfred. Chloe saw that she had taken off her gloves. Her big diamond ring sparkled in the sun as she picked up the reins, preparing to walk back up to the barn. "That pony belongs with an experienced rider," Mrs. Sloane muttered, as if talking to herself. But Chloe heard her, and so did everyone else. "Come along, Amandasue," Mrs. Sloane called. "We have to meet your daddy for lunch, then get you back here in time for your lesson. We don't want to keep Daddy waiting now, do we, sugar?"

Amanda didn't look at her mother, waiting by the in-gate. She put a hand on Jump For Joy's neck as if she were going to pat him, but she didn't pat him. She turned and headed slowly toward her mother, letting her hand trail lightly along the length of the pony's body all the way to his tail. Chloe felt Jump For Joy flinch when Amanda's hand brushed his flank. Amanda picked up a few strands of the pony's hair at the top of his tail and let her hand slide all the way to the ends of them before she let go. Then she marched toward her mother.

" 'Bye," Amanda said, not looking back at the group.

The other kids stared at Amanda walking away with her mother. The two were talking as they went up the hill, but no one could hear what they said. Once Chloe saw Amanda turn and look back at them. It gave her an uneasy feeling, but she tried to put it out of her head. Nothing was going to spoil this day!

"Walk him around for ten minutes or so, then you can bring him up," Sharon told her.

"Okay, Sharon," Chloe said. "Thank you for coming down to help."

"You're welcome," Sharon told her. "Come on, Earl," she called to the little dog. He trotted on his stubby legs after Sharon, who left the ring and headed up to the barn.

"I'll walk with you," Megan said to Chloe.

"Man, is it hot out here," Keith remarked.

"Let's go swimming in the lake!" Max suggested.

"Oh, I want to go, too," Megan said.

"Me, too," Chloe said.

"So come on," Max said.

"Can't you wait for me and Chloe to finish exercising Jump For Joy?" Megan asked.

"I guess," Max grumbled good-naturedly. "But Sharon said ten minutes. If we don't see you coming up to the barn in exactly ten minutes, we're going without you. I'm about to melt!"

"Okay, we'll see you in ten," Megan promised.

Chloe asked Jump For Joy to walk forward again, and Megan walked along beside them. The time passed quickly as the two girls slowly circled the spacious arena, talking and laughing. After they had been around six times, the ten minutes were up.

"Time to swim!" Megan said, checking her watch.

Chloe swung her legs over the saddle and slid very, very slowly to the ground. After finally riding her pony, she was reluctant to get off him. She ran up the stirrups and loosened the girth and, taking the reins over his head, began to lead the pony up the path toward the barn. As her worries about riding Jump For Joy had faded, she began to notice the heat. The sun seemed to pound on her head and shoulders as she trudged up the hill. Looping the reins around her elbow, she undid her helmet and pulled it off. Her pale blond hair was darkened with sweat and plastered to the sides of her face, which was flushed from the heat.

"Boy, that swim is sure going to feel good," Chloe remarked.

Megan helped Chloe untack Jump For Joy, who had only sweated a little under the saddle pad from his exercise. "You can brush him off when we get back," Megan told Chloe. "Come on, I can't wait to jump in that lake."

"Thanks for letting me use your chaps," Chloe said, unzipping them. She rolled them neatly and handed them to Megan.

"You're welcome," Megan said.

Keith and Max came to see if the girls were ready. "That's a first," Max remarked when he saw that they were. "I can't remember a single time in my whole life that I haven't had to wait for Megan."

"Let's go," Keith said.

"Did you tell somebody that we're going swimming in the lake?" Max asked Keith.

"I told Jake," Keith said. "He said he'd drive the truck up in a little while and pick us up." Jake was Sharon Wyndham's husband.

"Great!" Megan said.

"I'll brush you off as soon as I get back, I promise," Chloe said to Jump For Joy. She kissed his muzzle and slid the stall door closed.

The four kids were just starting out the back door when they heard Allie calling. "Hey!" her voice carried all the way from the main aisle in a tone that stopped them in their tracks. They waited while she strode toward them, arms swinging. "Where're y'all goin'?" she demanded.

"To the lake for a swim," Keith said.

"Did you tell anybody you were goin'?" Allie wanted to know.

"Sure, Allie. We told Jake. He's coming to pick us up in a little while," Max said.

Allie looked at Chloe. "Are your stalls done?" she asked.

Chloe cleaned her pony and Bo Peep's stalls every day. It was part of the agreement she had made with Sharon to work off the board on Jump For Joy. Usually she cleaned them first thing in the morning, as soon as she arrived at the barn. But today she had been busy with Dr. Pepper and then with riding Jump For Joy. So the stalls were not done yet. Chloe looked at Megan, at the barn floor, and finally at Allie. "No, but—" she started to say.

"Then you're not goin' anywhere," Allie said firmly.

"Al-lie," Megan pleaded.

69

"Aw, let her go, Allie," Keith said.

"I'll do them as soon as I get back," Chloe said earnestly. "I promise."

"And meanwhile, while you're up at the lake swimmin' and havin' fun, your pony has to stand in a dirty stall waitin' until you feel like cleanin' it?" Allie asked incredulously. She put her hands on the hips of her cutoffs and looked hard at Chloe.

"Please, Allie," Megan begged. "It's so hot. Let her do the stalls later. I'll help you clean them after we swim," Megan said to Chloe.

"No, I'll stay," Chloe told the other kids. "Allie's right. I should've done my chores first thing, but I was busy with Jump For Joy. He and Bo Peep shouldn't have to stand around in a dirty stall. I'll do them right now."

"We're only going to be up at the lake for an hour or so," Megan tried again. "Do your stalls as soon as we get back. You'll feel a lot cooler after a swim."

"No." Chloe shook her head. "I wouldn't enjoy the swim, anyway. Y'all go on without me. Maybe after I'm done I can meet you up at the lake." She knew Allie was right. Chloe was responsible for cleaning the two stalls, and they really couldn't wait. A horse couldn't understand that you would be back to clean his stall as soon as you took a little dip in the lake to cool off. A horse would just stand and suffer patiently in a dirty stall. Chloe

70

couldn't bear to think of either Jump For Joy or Bo Peep standing in muck, wondering who had forgotten to care for them.

"Don't worry, ponies, I'm coming," she said, starting back toward the main aisle. She thought of something she meant to tell Megan and turned around to say it, but the kids had already gone out the back door. Chloe heard them laughing faintly as she stuck her hands in her pockets and trudged toward the main aisle, where Bo Peep and Jump For Joy's stalls were.

6

CHLOE WENT AND GOT THE PITCHFORK, SET IT IN THE old blue wheelbarrow, and started toward Bo Peep's stall. Bo Peep was a medium-size Exmoor pony with a shiny, dark bay coat and a brown, mealy-colored muzzle. Her neck was a thick mass of muscle and mane that wobbled back and forth when she walked. Chloe had never seen such a wide neck on any horse or pony. The instructors at Thistle Ridge laughingly called her neck "the air-bag," because if a rider tipped forward on the pony, her fat neck cushioned him just like an airbag in a car! Chloe had often been grateful for Bo Peep's sturdy neck. As many times as she had been tossed forward by one of Bo Peep's famous bucks, she had recovered her balance by grabbing the pony's neck.

When Chloe entered Bo Peep's stall, the pony looked suspiciously over her shoulder at her, ears slightly back. Chloe knew that meant that she'd better not approach any further, or Bo Peep might kick at her. Chloe dug into her pocket and pulled out half a carrot. She snapped it in two and held out half in her hand invitingly. The pony pricked up her ears at the sound of the carrot breaking.

"Here, Peeps," Chloe said. "Come see what I've got for you." Bo Peep turned around and came to nibble the carrot. Chloe easily slipped the halter over her head. She led the pony out of the stall, put her on cross-ties, and pushed the wheelbarrow into the stall. Then she took the pitchfork and began picking up the piles of manure and wet bedding.

Mucking out stalls was one of the hardest chores in the stables, but Chloe actually enjoyed it. Whenever she had finished cleaning a stall, she got a feeling of great satisfaction, which didn't come with all jobs. Washing the dishes, for instance, was much easier. But, given a choice, Chloe would have taken stall cleaning over dish washing any day.

There was an art to cleaning a stall, just as there was a right way to do everything that had to do with horses. Chloe had learned that it was best to pick up as much muck with the fork as you could, while leaving as much of the dry bedding as possible. She lifted a pile and gave the pitchfork a couple of shakes, letting the dry wood shavings fall through the tines and back to the floor of the stall. Then she dumped the manure into the wheelbarrow.

Bo Peep was neat; most of her piles were in the same corner of her stall. And she never pooped in her water buckets, the way Prince Charming did. Bo Peep did scatter her hay all over her stall, though. That was because the pony liked to burrow her head under a pile of hay when she slept. The kids had often found the little mare snoozing away, her head buried under a mound of hay, snoring loudly! Chloe gathered the hay into a neat pile under the water buckets. Then she dug out the dry shavings from around the edges of the stall and spread them evenly, noticing that there was only enough bedding for a thin layer. It was time to put more shavings down.

Allie liked all her horses to have thick, soft bedding. Jake, Sharon's husband, would complain that the farm was spending a fortune on shavings, and Allie would counter, "If you skimp on shavings, you'll just be spendin' more on treatin' their feet for thrush, Jake." Chloe knew that thrush was a stinky infection horses got in their feet if they stood around in wet bedding.

She set the pitchfork aside and carefully backed the loaded wheelbarrow out of the stall. It was hard going; if you tilted the wheelbarrow just a little bit too much to the side, it would dump over, spilling the whole load. Chloe had done that more than once while learning to maneuver the heavy wheelbarrow.

She went slowly out the back door, working hard to keep the heavy wheelbarrow in balance. A little bumpy path led behind the old fence near where she had jogged Jump For Joy for the vet that morning. Beyond the fence the path ended in a drop-off, where the manure was dumped. Chloe tilted the wheelbarrow and dumped her load, holding the handles high and twisting it from side to side to get out every last bit. Then she pushed the empty wheelbarrow back along the path. It felt very light and jounced into the air whenever the tire hit a bump in the path.

Chloe set down the wheelbarrow just inside the barn door. Bales of wood shavings wrapped in brown paper were stacked there. She pulled one off the stack and wrestled the heavy bale into the wheelbarrow. She needed another, but she'd have to come back for it. The bales were too heavy for her to push two at a time. Chloe envied Allie, who saved herself trips by carrying three bales at once, stacked high in the wheelbarrow.

When she had fetched two bales, Chloe tore off the paper wrapping and began spreading the shavings with the pitchfork. When the bedding looked thick and fluffy enough, she piled the rest of the shavings around the edges of the stall. Then she threw away the crumpled paper wrapping and led Bo Peep into her freshly cleaned stall, smiling all the while, because she knew what would happen next.

Chloe slid the stall door closed, then peered through the bars surrounding the top of the stall. Bo Peep seemed excited. She put her nose down and sniffed at the clean shavings, then snorted loudly several times when sawdust tickled her nostrils. With her huge neck outstretched toward the floor, the pony spun quickly around and around in her stall, searching for just the right spot. Chloe giggled. She had seen Bo Peep do this over and over again, but it just got funnier every time. Through some mysterious logic all her own, the pony seemed to decide that the time was right and abruptly stopped turning around. She dropped to her knees, folded her haunches, and lay down. Then, quick as a cat, she rolled over on her back and began to wriggle around on the scratchy wood shavings.

Chloe laughed. "You silly girl," she said fondly to the pony.

Bo Peep gave a snort as if to reply, "You're silly. Don't you know how nice it is to have these shavings scratch my back? It feels sooooo good. Why don't you try it?" She went on rolling exuberantly. When she had finally had enough, she got her legs underneath her again, stood up, and shook long and hard, just like a dog after a bath. Shavings flew everywhere but mostly clung to Bo Peep's back, mane, and tail. Then the little mare sauntered over to her water bucket. Chloe watched the pony's throat bob as she swallowed the water in long gulps.

"I suppose you expect me to brush all those shavings off you, don't you, Miss Priss?" Chloe said to Bo Peep.

The pony just switched her tail and bent to nibble her hay. Feeling satisfied with her stall cleaning, Chloe wiped her sweaty, dusty forehead against her sleeve. Then she put the pitchfork in the wheelbarrow, rolled it down the aisle, and went to work on her own pony's stall.

It took two trips to the manure pile and three bales of shavings to get Jump For Joy's stall clean. Because the pony had been off work and spent so much time in the barn, his stall was much dirtier than Bo Peep's had been. Chloe had to hold her breath when she scooped out the muckiest stuff from the middle of the stall, where he'd peed. A strong, stinky ammonia smell came from the wet muck, and she hurried to cover it with dry shavings.

By the time she had finished, Chloe was dripping with sweat. Sawdust clung to her skin in a thin, itchy film, making her even hotter. She thought longingly of the cool lake as a trickle of sweat rolled down her cheek. If she hurried, she might still have time to enjoy a dip in the water with the other kids before they left the lake.

Chloe put Jump For Joy back into his stall and slipped off his leather halter. Jump For Joy gazed at her with his kind, dark eyes. His little ears were pricked forward intensely. He watched her go out of the stall and clip the webbed nylon stall guard closed. Chloe was about to hurry along so she could go swimming, but she was stopped by the sight of her adorable pony.

Jump For Joy nickered ever so softly and longingly, and Chloe felt her heart melting with love at the sight of him. She couldn't resist; she ducked back under the stall guard and went to his side. Chloe dug into her pocket and found one morsel of carrot, grown soft in the heat, but still sweet. She fed it to him, loving the feel of his muzzle, which was just exactly like soft velvet as he searched her hand for another treat.

"You're my pony, and I'll take care of you always," Chloe whispered to him. Jump For Joy stood very still, as if he were listening carefully to what she said. She put her mouth close to one of his ears and felt silky hair against her lips as she murmured lovingly, "And nobody will ever yank on your mouth or make you slip in the mud ever again." She felt a touch of anger as she remembered the careless handling Jump For Joy had endured when he had belonged to Amanda. "So don't you worry anymore. From now on you'll be safe and happy, I promise," Chloe finished, wrapping her arms around the pony's neck.

She rested her cheek against the pony's white fur, which felt cool in spite of the sticky heat of the day. Then she closed her eyes, imagining all the wonderful rides she would have on her very own pony, now that he was sound enough to carry her. They would go for bareback trail rides through the pastures and woods and hills of Thistle Ridge Farm. Riding her own pony, Chloe would enjoy her classes with Leigh a thousand times more than she already did. And of course Jump For Joy would jump again—Sharon had said so. Chloe felt certain that if she continued to take good care of him, he would be just as good a jumper as he had been before the accident—even better, she decided. They would win blue ribbons and championships in every horse show. Everyone who saw them would know that Chloe and Jump For Joy belonged together.

If she ever grew too big to ride him, or he got too old to be ridden, she would let him live in one of the pastures at Thistle Ridge. He could run free all day with the other old school horses, who had served for many years teaching people to ride and earned their retirement. Chloe knew she would never, ever sell Jump For Joy, the way some kids sold their outgrown ponies. "You'll be mine forever," she said to him. She gave him a final loving pat and reluctantly started to leave. She was just about to duck under the stall guard when she heard the Sloanes approaching.

"Take one look at this pony, Gerald, and tell me he doesn't belong with our Mandy." Mrs. Sloane's nasal drawl cut through the humid air.

Chloe froze. She flattened herself against the front wall inside the stall and prayed that the Sloanes wouldn't notice her there. If Mrs. Sloane was unpleasant, Mr. Sloane was a monster. Chloe knew she was old enough not to be frightened by adults, but she had never met anyone like Amanda's father. He terrified her.

"Pamela, I don't have time to be lookin' at horses all afternoon. I've got to be at a meeting in twenty minutes," Mr. Sloane said.

"This'll only take a minute, Gerald," Mrs. Sloane said soothingly.

"All right, Pamela, where's the pony?" Mr. Sloane barked.

"He's over here, right in this stall," Mrs. Sloane replied.

Their voices came through the bars surrounding the top of the stall, just above Chloe's head. She closed her eyes and tried not to move so much as a hair. Luckily, she was small for her age and

80

couldn't be seen over the wooden wall that enclosed the bottom half of the stall. She breathed silently through her mouth, hoping they wouldn't decide to go into the stall.

"Now, Pamela, tell me what on earth is so special about this scrawny little ol' pony? Amanda's got herself a nice big horse. Why, that Prince Charming is Olympic quality. You know the only reason he's not on the United States Equestrian Team right now is because I bought him," Mr. Sloane said.

Amanda's plaintive voice came from the other side of the wall. "But, Daddy, Prince Charming is *hard* to ride. How can I compete in an important show like the Charity Classic if I have to *think* the whole time I'm riding? Jump For Joy is easy to ride. If I'm on him in the Charity Classic, I'll be *sure* to win it. Don't you want to see me win in a great big show like that?" Amanda wheedled.

Chloe couldn't believe what she was hearing. What was Amanda talking about? How could she think that Chloe would let her ride Jump For Joy? After all, the Sloanes had been happy to get rid of him when his leg was injured. They would have let him die. Chloe scowled. *Jump For Joy is my pony now,* she thought. *And I'll never let Amanda ride him. Not in the Charity Classic. Not anywhere. And no one can make me.* She crossed her arms, feeling mad enough to come out and

say so to the Sloanes. She pictured herself standing right up to mean Mrs. Sloane and bossy,
spoiled Amanda. She would tell them that they
should have appreciated Jump For Joy when he
was theirs and that now it was too late. But Gerald Sloane's voice stopped her.

"Well, now, of course I want you to win, sugar
pie," Mr. Sloane said to Amanda. Chloe had never
heard Mr. Sloane speak tenderly to his daughter
or to anybody. "And you will—on Prince
Charming."

"But, Daddy, I don't want to ride Prince Charming. I want to ride Jump For Joy. Please, Daddy,"
Amanda cajoled, "get him back for me." Her voice
was as sweet as honeysuckle.

"Gerald, the child will win on this pony. I really
think we should get him back for our Amandasue,"
Mrs. Sloane added.

"But, Pamela, this pony has a busted-up leg," Mr.
Sloane said. "He can't even jump."

"Oh, yes, he can," Mrs. Sloane insisted. "I heard
Sharon say so just this morning. She said there was
no reason why he couldn't start jumping again, as
long as his legs are kept wrapped."

"Is that so?" Mr. Sloane sounded interested for a
change, instead of just impatient. Suddenly Chloe's
anger turned to uneasiness, then fear. She felt a
wave of sickness wash over her as Mrs. Sloane
went on.

"Who would have thought he'd ever make such a recovery, as lame as he was?" Mrs. Sloane mused. "But it seems he's just as good as he was before. Maybe even better," she added. "Just look at that fine animal, and I'm sure you'll agree with me. I know what an eye for horses you have, Gerald."

"Now that *is* true," Mr. Sloane agreed. "I do have an eye for fine horseflesh."

"Then surely you can see that this animal is quality. And he belongs with Amanda," Mrs. Sloane continued. "It would be a shame to deprive our Mandy of the experience of winning the Short Stirrup division at the Charity Classic horse show."

"Weeell . . ." Mr. Sloane said.

"Please, Daddy?" Amanda's voice was just the right mixture of pathetic and hopeful. "I want my pony back." Chloe heard her let out a little, hiccuping sob.

"Now, Mandy honey, don't cry, sugar. Daddy didn't know you wanted this pony so much. We'll see about gettin' him back right away," Mr. Sloane said to her. "Now can I go, Pamela?" Mr. Sloane asked in his familiar, loud, irritated voice. "It is so dad-gum hot in this barn. I got to get to the air-conditionin'!" he exclaimed, his voice getting further away as he spoke.

"Of course, Gerald. I knew if you took just one

look at this pony, you would agree with me. I'll see you at dinner," Mrs. Sloane called after him. "Now then, Amanda," Mrs. Sloane said in a bright, cheery tone, "Daddy's goin' to get your pony back. Aren't you happy?"

Amanda answered her mother in a pouty, surly voice. "I want to ride him *now*," she said.

"Just as soon as he's yours again, Amanda," Mrs. Sloane said.

"Well, what if they won't sell him back to us?"

"Everything's for sale, Sugarpie," Mrs. Sloane assured her daughter. "Now go get Prince Charming, and get ready for your lesson. You have fifteen minutes to get down to the ring. We don't want to keep Sharon waiting, now, do we?"

"I don't want to ride Prince Charming any-more," Chloe heard Amanda grumbling as she and Mrs. Sloane moved away from Jump For Joy's stall. When their footsteps had faded, Chloe slumped against the wall, feeling relieved. Then she remembered what Mr. Sloane had said about trying to get Jump for Joy back for Amanda, and the queasy uneasiness returned. The Sloanes had so much money, they were used to buying what-ever they wanted. Could they buy Jump For Joy back, even if Chloe refused to sell him? She didn't know. But she knew Mr. Sloane was a powerful man. Amanda was used to getting everything she wanted. And Mr. Sloane was used to getting it for her.

"Well, they're not getting you back," Chloe said to Jump For Joy. "They can't buy everything." She hugged her pony fiercely around his neck, then ducked under the stall guard and marched out the barn door, heading for the pasture.

7

CHLOE DIDN'T KNOW WHAT TO DO, BUT SHE KNEW SOME-
one who would. Even when things seemed impossible, Megan always came up with a plan. *I can't let
the Sloanes take my pony from me*, Chloe thought,
walking as fast as she could through the stiff, knee-
high grass toward the lake. *Megan will know what
to do.*

The August heat shimmered in waves over the
ground. Chloe felt the thick, dry grass stems poking
the bottoms of her feet through the worn leather
soles of her paddock boots. She lifted her feet high
with each step, to keep the sharp stalks from
scratching her bare legs. She felt very small as she
trudged through the wide pasture all alone. Every
growing thing that had been a bright, lush green

the month before had begun to acquire a coppery golden sheen from baking in the hot sun. Even the grasshoppers had turned from vivid green to a grayish brown. They went zizzing away from her in every direction as she trudged steadily toward the wooded hill that hid the lake.

Soon the ground began to tilt uphill, and Chloe was forced to walk a little more slowly. The hot, moist air seemed to press against her as she made her way up the hill. She had to change her path often to avoid the waist-high, prickly thistles that clumped all over the hillside. Their pinkish purple flowers sat prim and protected above the jagged, barbed leaves and stems. No animal could chew those tough plants, Chloe knew. "Ouch," she said, having accidentally swiped her ankle against a thistle leaf. *I wish I were a thistle*, Chloe thought. *I'd stick that Amanda Sloane right in the butt!*

At last she had climbed the hill and entered the pine woods. No breeze found its way into the shade there, but at least she was out of the hot sun. Chloe quickened her pace, hearing the sound of her steps change as her feet crunched on the brown needles piled thick under the pine trees. She noticed the persistent rapping of a woodpecker somewhere nearby. Out of habit she looked around and spotted his red-crested head. He perched on the trunk of a pine tree, busily drilling holes to trap his dinner. Ordinarily, Chloe would have stopped to watch him. She was always fascinated by animals. But this time she hurried on, anxious to reach the other children. She heard the woodpecker stop in surprise as she drew close, then resume his pecking when she was past.

In another moment the sound of splashing and shouts and laughter drifted through the trees. Chloe hurried out of the pine woods and into the clearing, where a large, sparkling blue lake defied the summer heat, cooled by the underground springs that fed it. Sand had been dumped along one edge of the lakeshore, making a beach for swimming and sunbathing. Nearby was a wooden dock made of silvery gray cedar that reached several yards out into the lake. The other three members of the Short Stirrup Club were taking turns jumping off the dock into the water.

"Okay, watch this, you guys." Megan's happy voice carried above the lapping of the lake water and the boys' laughter. "This is going to be a perfect cannonball," she announced.

Chloe watched as Megan took a running start, her bare feet pounding over the weathered boards. She leaped as high as she could out over the water. She grabbed her knees to tuck, but one hand must have slipped. Chloe saw Megan's arms wave frantically for a moment as she sprawled into the lake with a mighty splash. She came to the surface, coughing and spluttering, as the boys howled with laughter.

"That was a perfect belly flop!" Max crowed.

"I bet I made the biggest splash, though!" Megan countered. She crawled slowly up the ladder and sat on the edge of the dock, panting.

Chloe hurried over to her and asked, "Are you okay?"

Giggling, Megan nodded, and said, "Did you see that?"

"Yeah, I was afraid you'd hurt yourself," Chloe said.

"Nah," Megan said. "I just got water up my nose, that's all," she said, wriggling it and wiping at it. I'm glad you made it. Where's your swimsuit?"

"I forgot it," Chloe said, sitting down at the edge of the dock next to Megan. "I'll just swim in my clothes. I don't care if they get wet. It's so hot." She began unlacing her paddock boots.

"Did you finish your stalls?" Megan asked, swinging her feet in the cool water.

"Yeah. Megan, listen. Something happened. . . ." Chloe told Megan what the Sloanes had said about getting Jump For Joy. "What do you think I should do?" Chloe finished anxiously.

"Nothing," Megan said. "Don't even think twice about it. For one thing, you have his registration papers, remember? Mr. Sloane signed them over to you that day they were going to—" Megan broke off. Nobody liked to remember the day Jump For Joy had almost lost his life. "Anyway," Megan went on, "the papers are in your name now. The Sloanes can't buy him if you won't sell him. And another thing—even if they could, the Short Stirrup Club will stand by you. You've waited a long time and worked so hard to have a pony of your own. Nobody can take that away from you."

"Not even Mr. Sloane?" Chloe asked doubtfully.

Megan shook her head firmly. "Not even Mr. Sloane. Now quit worrying about it. In fact," Megan said mischievously, "why don't you go jump in the lake!" She gave Chloe a playful shove. Chloe squealed as she lost her balance. She grabbed at Megan's arm, and both girls fell off the dock and into the lake.

Chloe gasped as she hit the cool water. Then she and Megan tussled, laughing as they tried to splash each other with torrents of lake water. Chloe felt the heat and worry of the day wash away with the sweat and dirt as she swam. Surrounded by good friends, she didn't feel so threatened. "I'd like to tell that mean Mr. Sloane to go jump in the lake!" Chloe said.

Suddenly something grabbed her by the ankles and tugged. Chloe went under. She came up and saw that it was Keith who had dunked her. "I'll get you, Keith Bradley Hill," she yelled, lunging after him.

"Oh, yeah?" Keith taunted. "Let's see you try!" He swiped his arm across the water, dousing Chloe with a sheet of spray.

"Hey!" Chloe protested. She had to stop and wipe her eyes before she could go after him. When she opened her eyes, she saw Keith go under suddenly. He came up, shaking his head, water streaming over his face and from his longish, black hair. Chloe realized what had happened to Keith when Megan came up beside him, laughing.

"Got you!" Megan yelled at Keith. She swam over to Chloe and the girls high-fived.

"Thanks, Meg!" Chloe said to her friend.

"My pleasure," Megan said, grinning at Keith.

"Megan?" Chloe said, treading water, "are you really, really sure I don't have to worry about losing Jump For Joy?"

"I'm positive," Megan said. "Now quit being so serious. You're always worrying about something. Just have some fun for a change."

Chloe smiled. "Okay," she said. "I guess you're right."

So Chloe concentrated on having fun. The cool lake was delightful after the long, hot day. She swam and played with her friends, and soon she had forgotten all about the Sloanes.

After another fifteen minutes in the water, the low thrum of an engine caught the attention of the children. When they looked up, Jake Wyndham's blue Ford pickup truck was just appearing over the hill, jouncing over clumps of bitterweed as it rolled toward them. The kids waved enthusiastically at Jake, who raised two fingers from the steering wheel in a dignified salute. When he had reached the lakeshore, he threw up the gearshift and switched off the ignition.

"Hey, Jake!" Keith yelled from the water. "Why don't you come swimming with us?"

Jake got out of the truck and strolled down to the beach. He lifted his Atlanta Braves baseball cap and smoothed back his thinning, sandy hair. Jake always wore blue jeans and cowboy boots, no matter how hot it was. Chloe simply could not imagine him in a swimsuit.

"I'm not exactly dressed for swimmin', Keith," he said, his friendly blue eyes twinkling.

"Aw, who cares?" Keith said.

"Yeah, just swim in your clothes," Max said.

"Nope," Jake shook his head slowly. "Are y'all about ready to come back to the barn?"

"I am," Megan said.

"Me too," Chloe said.

"I'm not!" Max and Keith said at the same time.

"Well, this train is leavin'," Jake said, jerking his thumb in the direction of his pickup truck. "Anybody who wants a ride better come now."

"Coming," the girls said, wading toward the sandy beach.

"Oh, okay," the boys grumbled, splashing through the shallows to the shore.

The dripping children gathered their shoes and clambered into the back of the pickup truck while Jake got in the front. Chloe and Megan sat side by side on the spare tire, while the boys each took a seat on the metal hubs over the rear wheels. Chloe could feel the hot tire through her wet shorts. The truck moved off down the hill, its springs squeaking in protest at the bumpy ground. When they reached the smooth stretch at the bottom of the hill, Jake drove a little faster. The air moved pleasantly across their faces, drying their hair and clothes. Chloe closed her eyes, enjoying the short drive. It was always fun to ride in the back of a pickup truck.

"So what's the school like here?" Megan said to Chloe.

"Yeah, tell us about it," Max said to Keith. "We start next week, don't we?"

"Monday morning," Keith said. He made a face. "I'm not ready to go back to school yet. It seems like summer should last a lot longer."

"Yeah, I can't believe school starts in August down here," Max complained. "In Connecticut we didn't start school until almost the middle of September."

"My dad says it's because in the old days there were so many kids who had to work on their families' farms. So school started in August and was let out in May, before planting time," Keith explained. "The farmers all needed their kids to help with the crops."

"Yeah, at least we'll get out earlier," Megan said. "In Connecticut we didn't get out of school until nearly the end of June."

"I suppose that's fair," Max mused. "It just so hot now! I can't imagine putting on school clothes in this weather."

"Oh, it's not so bad in school," Keith told them.

"Yeah," Chloe added. "At least now we have air-conditioning."

"You mean, your school didn't used to have air-conditioning?" Max asked incredulously.

"Not until last year," Chloe said.

"Are you allowed to wear shorts, at least?" Max said.

"Nope," Chloe said.

"Wow, I don't know how you could stand it. What did you do?" Megan asked.

"We sweated!" Chloe and Keith said together. Then they laughed.

"At least we'll be sixth graders this year," Keith said. "We'll be the biggest kids in Hickoryville Elementary."

"I guess that'll be good," Megan said. They were within sight of the barn now, near the back side of the smaller outdoor ring. "Oh, look! That's Prince

Charming." She pointed to the big gray horse. Amanda Sloane was having her lesson with Sharon. "Look at him trot. Isn't he a gorgeous mover?" Megan said dreamily, leaning across Chloe's lap so she could see better.

"I still don't get it," Max said. "What is so great about Prince Charming?"

"You obviously have no taste in horses," Megan said disdainfully to her brother. "Prince Charming is fabulous." She sighed wistfully. "I wish I could ride him again."

"Didn't you learn your lesson the last time you rode him?" Max said.

"Yeah, remember how he jumped you right out of the warm-up ring and into the hunter ring at the horse show," Chloe reminded her, "just as that other rider was jumping around? And they had to stop her round to wait for you to get out of the ring. Boy, was she mad. Remember how you said you were never going to ride anyone except Pixie from then on?"

"Yeah, but that was almost a month ago," Megan waved a hand impatiently. "I'm a much better rider now. I could handle him just fine."

"Gosh, Megan, you're so loyal," Max teased. "Next thing you know, you're going to leave the Short Stirrup Club to be friends with Amanda just so you can ride her horse."

"Well, someone ought to ride him," Megan countered. "Amanda sure can't."

"Oh!" Chloe said. She grabbed Megan's arm and pointed to the arena, where a moment ago they had seen Amanda trotting around on her horse.

"What is it?" Megan asked.

"Look!" Chloe insisted.

"Where? I don't see— Oh . . . my . . . gosh." Megan stood up, forgetting she was in the back of a bouncy truck. She immediately tumbled to the bed of the pickup as Jake hit the gas and steered toward the arena gate.

"Holy cow!" Max said.

Amanda had been trotting toward a small jump when Prince Charming swerved away from it at the last second. Amanda had lost her balance and toppled over the right side of her horse. Chloe cringed, waiting to see Amanda hit the dirt, but she didn't.

"Where is she?" Megan said, looking for Amanda on the ground as the truck approached the ring.

They heard Sharon shout, "Let go, Amanda! Let go!" and then saw her scurry toward the horse.

Prince Charming turned and headed for the in gate. Then they finally saw what had happened to Amanda. Though she was out of the saddle, she hadn't fallen off because she was hanging on to Prince's right side!

Amanda screamed a piercing scream as she hung

spread-eagle from one rein and one stirrup. Her other arm and leg hung toward the ground, dangerously close to being trampled by Prince's trotting hooves.

"Amanda, let go!" Sharon called urgently.

"She's hanging on to the rein. That's why she hasn't fallen," Megan said. "Why doesn't she just let go?"

"No, look," Chloe said. "Her foot is caught in the stirrup! If she lets go, she'll be dragged!" Safety stirrups came with a quick-release rubber band on one side that was designed to snap in just such an emergency. All the kids at Thistle Ridge rode with safety stirrups. But not Amanda. Amanda's expensive Hermes saddle was fitted with shiny, solid stirrup irons, the best that money could buy. Her foot had slipped all the way through the stirrup when she fell off the saddle. Now she was caught, hanging by her ankle, unable to fall free of the horse. Chloe realized that Amanda was in serious danger.

Prince had stopped for a moment. He seemed perplexed by the rider hanging from his off side. He kept turning slowly to the right, as if trying to get a good look at the situation so he could figure out how to dislodge his rider. Amanda kept letting out earsplitting shrieks, one after the other. Sharon must have seen what the problem was by then. She was walking toward Prince Charming as fast as she could, without scaring him. "Amanda, just be still," she called. "Please don't scream! I'm coming to help you."

But Prince had figured out that he had once again unseated his young rider. The pasture sprawled invitingly, full of tasty grass, just beyond the arena fence. There was no way Prince was going to let Sharon catch him before he had gone out for a good graze. Chloe could have sworn Prince gave a little shrug of his shoulders, as if to say, "Oh, well. If you won't get off, I guess you'll just have to come along with me." He gave up circling Amanda and cantered toward the in gate.

"Whoa!" Sharon yelled desperately as Prince sped by her, dodging her outstretched hand as she tried to catch his reins.

"Oh, poor Amanda," Chloe said.

"He'll jump the gate!" Megan said. "He'll jump anything."

"He won't have to. Look, it's open!" Keith said, pointing. Indeed, the gate was ajar, just wide enough for a horse to slip through.

"Jaaake!" Sharon hollered, seeing the blue truck approaching. She gestured frantically toward Prince Charming. The truck had a chance of cutting off the horse's escape if Jake could beat Prince to the gate. Jake gunned the engine, and Chloe grabbed the sides of the spare tire as the truck surged forward. Keith slid off the hub to the truck bed and stayed there, where there was no danger of falling out. Max scooted down beside him. They all watched Prince galloping toward the open gate with the screaming Amanda attached to his side. The truck was almost there.

"We're going to make it!" Max said excitedly.

"I hope you're right," Keith said.

For a moment it did seem that the truck would beat the horse to the gate and block his escape. But then somehow, just as Jake was nearly there, Prince took four quick strides and ducked through the opening, springing past the truck just a second before it would have cut him off.

Amanda let loose a long wail of desperation as Prince Charming galloped off toward the back pasture, dragging her through the thistles as he went.

8

CHLOE STARED IN HORROR AT THE SIGHT OF AMANDA, still hanging by her foot and clinging to the right rein, flopping along on the horse's side.

Jake stuck his head out the open window of the truck and yelled, "You kids hang on back there!" He whipped the truck around, its old springs creaking and complaining, and sped through the pasture after Prince Charming. The children sat on the floor of the truck bed, gripping the sides of the truck as they bounced crazily over the bumpy ground.

Chloe kept her eye on Amanda. It seemed like forever, but really it was only a few moments before Amanda's foot finally slipped free of the stirrup somehow. Both her feet hit the ground, slowing

Prince, and Amanda let go of the rein. Chloe saw Amanda's seat go over her head in a somersault before she landed in a tangled heap. A little cloud of dust drifted away from where she had landed, following on Prince Charming's heels as he cantered casually toward the back pasture.

The truck pulled up beside Amanda a second later, and Jake leaped out and ran to her. Chloe, Megan, Max, and Keith scrambled out of the back as fast as they could. Amanda didn't make a sound for a moment. She lay sprawled on her stomach, face down, a sprig of yellow bitterweed clinging to one of her braids.

"Amanda, honey, are you okay?" Jake asked anxiously. He crouched by her side, trying to see her face. He looked like he wanted to pick her up, but was afraid to touch her; his hand hovered nervously near her shoulder. "Amanda?" he said again.

Amanda's fall was the most spectacular Chloe had ever seen. She was worried that Amanda hadn't survived to tell about it. "Is she alive?" Chloe asked, terrified. She was almost afraid to look closely at Amanda, who was as lifeless as a rag doll tossed aside.

"Is she unconscious?" Megan asked.

"Amanda, honey, talk," Jake pleaded. "Can you talk?"

For a second, Amanda didn't move. Then she slowly raised her head and opened her light blue eyes. She drew in a deep breath, then began to wail like a police siren. "Hooooooo," Amanda cried.

Jake seemed relieved. He patted her shoulder awkwardly, and said, "Now, then, Amanda. Don't cry like that. You'll be all right."

Amanda pushed herself to a sitting position and let out another wail. "Are you hurt anywhere, Amanda?" Jake asked her.

Amanda seemed to be considering. At last she wiped her eyes and tried to stop crying. "N-nooooo," she said piteously, her down-turned mouth trembling.

"That's good," Jake said, sounding genuinely glad. Amanda had one long scratch across her cheek, where a thistle barb had raked her, but otherwise looked unhurt. "Come get in the truck, and we'll drive you back to the barn," Jake said, helping her to her feet. Amanda was still breathing in jerky little hiccups as she walked slowly toward the pickup.

"What about Prince Charming?" Megan asked. "Shouldn't we try to catch him? It'll be dark soon."

At the mention of her horse's name, Amanda started to cry again. "I hope he gets lost!" she sobbed. "I'm never riding him again!"

Chloe shot Megan a worried look at that, but Megan didn't see. She had hurried over to Amanda and put an arm around her shoulders as she tried to console the shaken girl. Chloe felt the tiniest

102

twinge of envy when she saw her best friend's arm around Amanda Sloane. But then she dismissed it and hurried to Amanda's other side to see if she could help, too.

Max opened the passenger door of the truck for Amanda, who climbed in and sat down, still crying. He slammed the door and the other kids climbed in back. Jake turned the truck around and they drove to the stables.

Sharon was waiting anxiously by the arena. She shielded her eyes with a hand, watching as the truck rolled toward her. "Is she all right, Jake?" Sharon asked, looking across the driver's seat at the sniveling Amanda.

"I reckon so," Jake said. "She's not hurt, just that little ol' scratch on her cheek is all. But she is lucky," he added.

"Did you see which way the horse went?" Sharon asked.

"I don't care where he is! I hope he's lost for good!" Amanda sobbed angrily. "I'm never getting on him again." Her dirty face was flushed and striped with tear stains.

"Now, Amanda, you don't mean that," Sharon chided her gently. "You're just feeling upset because you fell off. That was a freak accident. Nothing like that will happen again, especially if we replace your stirrups with quick-release stirrups. Tomorrow is a new day. I tell you what; I have a little time in the morning because one of my steady students is away for the week. How about if I schedule a special lesson for you, bright and early, just to get you back up on Prince again?" Sharon said cheerfully.

Amanda shook her head vehemently. "No!" she insisted. "I hope he's lost forever. I'm not going near him ever again." She crossed her arms in fury and turned to Jake. "Take me back to the barn right now," she demanded. "I want to go hooooome." Amanda's words ended in another wailing sob as the tears began to stream down her face again.

At her own home that night, Chloe stirred her dinner absently with her fork, instead of eating it. No matter how hard she tried, she couldn't stop thinking about the events of the day. She had an uneasy feeling that the Sloanes might indeed find a way to get Jump For Joy back, in spite of what Megan had said. Chloe was especially worried after the way Amanda had acted when she fell off Prince Charming. That had been really scary, Chloe had to admit. She wasn't so sure she would want to get back on Prince Charming, either, if it had happened to her. She hoped that Amanda would somehow get over her fear and that Sharon would talk her into riding Prince again. But a little, nagging voice inside Chloe kept whispering, *What if she won't ride Prince anymore?*

"Chloe!"

Startled by her mother's voice, Chloe dropped her fork on the plate with a clatter. Her baby brother, Michael, began to cry, frightened by the sudden loud noise.

"I'm sorry, Michael. Please don't cry," Chloe said, making a funny face to amuse him.

The little boy stopped crying, but his lip poked out in a tired pout and tears glistened in his eyes. Chloe's mother stood up from the table and lifted him out of his booster seat. Michael clung to his mother's neck as she rubbed his back soothingly. "I called your name three times," Ms. Goodman said, frowning at her daughter.

"Sorry, Mama," Chloe said. "What did you say? I didn't hear you."

Ms. Goodman shook her head. "You're a thousand miles away today. I asked how your pony was."

"Fine," Chloe said. Before she could tell her mother about riding Jump For Joy, Ms. Goodman went on.

"You begged me to fix you macaroni and cheese for dinner, and you haven't touched one single bite. What on earth is the matter with you?" Ms. Goodman said. "And by the way," she added, before Chloe could answer, "you promised to do the wash yesterday, and not one load of it is done. Michael hasn't got a clean shirt to his name."

105

"I'm sorry, Mama," Chloe said sincerely. Her mother's eyes looked red and tired from working so many hours. Chloe remembered guiltily that she was supposed to do the laundry days ago but had been putting it off all week.

"You have very few responsibilities around this house," her mother continued. "I don't ask you to do very much, but when I do ask you to do a chore, I expect you to see that it gets done. And not four days later, after I've had to remind you ten times," she admonished. "You're old enough to help out around here. If you can't keep up with a few simple chores, then you're going to have to stop spending so much time at that barn," Ms. Goodman warned.

"I'll do it right away," Chloe promised. She picked up her fork and took three quick bites of her supper, washing them down with the rest of her milk. Then she quickly stood up and began to clear the table.

"I would appreciate that," Ms. Goodman said quietly. "I'm going to put Michael to bed."

"No bed, nooo," Michael whined as he was carried down the hall. His crying reminded Chloe of Amanda, and she began to worry all over again as she carried the dishes to the sink.

The rest of the week, Chloe made sure to do whatever she could to help out her mother at home. At the barn Chloe cleaned her stalls and

Sharon's tack and did whatever other barn chores Allie gave her. She rode Jump For Joy every day, and he was just as much a joy to ride as his name suggested. Chloe would have been completely happy, except for a couple of things that happened at the barn that week.

For one thing, Amanda still wouldn't ride Prince Charming. In spite of Amanda's wishes, Jake had retrieved the wayward horse the same evening he escaped. But no matter how her parents threatened and cajoled her, and however Sharon reasoned with her, Amanda staunchly refused to get back on her horse.

Every time Chloe rode Jump For Joy, though, Amanda would appear. She'd sit on the fence rail, a moody, pensive expression on her face, as she watched Chloe walk and trot around the ring. Chloe wished Amanda would go away. It made her nervous to have Amanda stare at her whenever she rode Jump For Joy.

Another thing that worried Chloe was that Megan was acting strangely. She had hardly spoken to Chloe all week. In fact, Chloe noticed, every since Amanda had fallen off Prince, Megan had been hanging around with Amanda. She had seen the two girls sitting on the picnic table in the courtyard, drinking sodas and talking. Chloe couldn't help wondering what that was all about. Usually Megan couldn't stand to be around Amanda.

Chloe and Megan had planned to have an end-of-summer sleep-over at the Morrisons' house that weekend, the last one before school began. They had talked about it the week before. But when Chloe reminded Megan about the sleep-over, Megan dismissed her.

"Oh, I forgot all about that. But anyway, I don't think I'll have time. I'm schooling Prince Charming for the Sloanes, so I'll be really busy with two horses to exercise," Megan said, and breezed by Chloe to tack up Prince Charming. Chloe wondered if she had done something to make Megan angry at her, but she couldn't think what it would be.

Things weren't any better when school began. Chloe and Megan had hoped to have the same homeroom. But the way things ended up, Megan, Max, and Keith got the same homeroom teacher while Chloe ended up in the dreaded Ms. Hood's homeroom. "Oh, no," Chloe groaned when she saw her schedule. "Ms. Margaret is the meanest teacher in the whole school!"

"Too bad," Keith said sympathetically. "My big sister, Haley, had Ms. Margaret when she was in the sixth grade. She's so mean and nasty, nobody can stand her." Keith lowered his voice as he added, "You know what the big kids call her? 'The Maggot.' " Keith and Max giggled, but Chloe was too dismayed to enjoy the joke. Why couldn't she have been in kind Mrs. East's room with the rest of the Short Stirrup Club?

Chloe also hadn't counted on all the homework the sixth graders got. The very first day of school she had an hour and a half of homework! It wasn't going to be easy, keeping up with her schoolwork, her barn chores, and her chores at home. By the end of the week, Chloe had the unhappy feeling that the sixth grade was going to be much harder than she had expected.

To make matters even worse, on Friday night, when Chloe got home from the barn, her mom was waiting to talk with her. "I got an interesting phone call today, Chloe," she said, "from Gerald Sloane."

Chloe felt her heart skip a beat as her mother went on. "He wanted to know if you would sell Jump For Joy back to him," Ms. Goodman said.

"What did you tell him?" Chloe asked in a panic. "You didn't say yes, did you?"

Her mother paused. "I told him you'd consider it," she said. She took a deep breath and said slowly, "Chloe, he offered twenty thousand dollars for the pony."

"I don't care!" Chloe declared. "Jump For Joy is not for sale!"

"Chloe, honey, just think for a minute. Twenty thousand dollars is an awful lot of money, more than I make in a whole year. That much money could pay for your college education."

"I make good grades. I'll get a scholarship to college," Chloe countered.

Ms. Good man sighed. "Honey, it's just so expensive to keep a pony."

"My pony doesn't cost you anything," Chloe protested. "I work off his board."

"Yes, and you're so busy working off your pony's board, you end up not doing your work at home." Ms. Goodman put her hands on her hips and reminded Chloe, "You were supposed to do the dishes after school, and they're still sitting in the sink."

Chloe shoved her hands in her pockets and stared at her worn tennis shoes. She had been in such a hurry to finish her homework after school so she could get to the barn, that she had forgotten to wash the dishes. "I'm sorry," Chloe said. "I'll do them now." She started for the kitchen, but her mother stopped her.

"Chloe, listen," Ms. Goodman said. "With twenty thousand dollars, we could pay off the mortgage on this house. If we did that, I could quit working so many hours at the Beacon and finish getting my realtor's license. Then I could pay you back the twenty thousand dollars when I start making commissions from selling real estate. We'd all be better off. And then you could buy another pony," Ms. Goodman pointed out. "Any pony you like."

"I don't want another pony," Chloe cried. "I want

Jump For Joy. I've wanted him ever since the first time I saw him, and now that I finally have him, I'm not letting mean old Mr. Sloane take him back just because he's rich. Amanda Sloane doesn't love Jump For Joy. It's her fault her was lame in the first place. I *love* Jump For Joy," Chloe said fiercely. "And he loves me. I promised him I'd take care of him forever and ever. I don't care how much money Mr. Sloane will pay. Jump For Joy is not for sale, do you hear me? Not for a million, billion dollars!"

Chloe was crying as she ran down the hall to the kitchen. She was angry that her mother would even suggest that she sell her beloved pony. At the same time she was terrified that her mom might *make* her sell Jump For Joy. She knew her mother's argument about the money was logical, but Chloe didn't feel logical. She just felt hurt. Suddenly, she wanted her grandmother. She yanked open the kitchen door and ran out into the carport.

It was past sunset, and the carport was in shadows. Before she could stop, Chloe felt her feet skidding on something spilled on the floor of the carport. Instantly, she realized she had forgotten to feed the animals that morning. Her dog, Jenny, must have gotten into the dog food and scattered it everywhere. In that same instant, Chloe slipped on the spilled dog food and fell flat on the concrete. Pain shot through her right arm as it smacked the

111

hard floor. It hurt so much that for a moment she could hardly breathe. Then she wanted to scream, but all she could do was gasp. Somehow, she managed to get up and stagger back into the kitchen. "Mama," Chloe managed to call. "I think I broke my arm."

9

MAMAW DROVE OVER AND PICKED UP MICHAEL SO THAT
Chloe's mother could take her to the emergency
room. On the way to the hospital, Chloe's arm hurt
worse than anything she had ever felt before. Try
as she might, she couldn't find a comfortable position for the injured arm. Wherever she held it, it
hurt just as much. Finally, she just cradled it lightly
against her waist with her other hand. Kathryn
Goodman drove tensely, her head craned toward
the windshield. She kept glancing over at Chloe, to
see how she was doing. Chloe gritted her teeth and
stayed silent the whole way to the hospital, though
the tears kept welling up and spilling soundlessly
from her eyes.

It was a twenty-minute drive to the new medical

center in Memphis. Chloe's mom helped her inside, and they checked in at the front desk. They answered a few questions, then sat down to wait for the doctor to come and X-ray Chloe's arm.

"How are you, honey?" her mother asked, pushing a strand of Chloe's pale blond hair back and tucking it behind her ear.

Chloe closed her eyes for a second, grateful for her mother's soothing hand. Then she looked at her mom and with great effort managed to fake a small smile. "Fine," Chloe said.

"You know, this could take a very long time," Ms Goodman said. She sighed and looked around the waiting room. There were several people who had come in ahead of them.

Just then a tall, slender woman with straight, ash blond hair strode into the waiting area. The woman wore blue jeans underneath a hospital scrub shirt and a stethoscope around her neck. Chloe recognized the woman instantly. It was Dr. Rose Morrison, Megan and Max's mother. She raised her good arm in a tiny, polite wave.

"Chloe!" Dr. Morrison exclaimed when she realized who was waving to her. Sounding concerned, she asked, "What happened to you?" She came over and knelt by Chloe, who showed her her arm and explained what had happened.

Dr. Morrison examined Chloe's arm, asking her a few questions about where it hurt and whether

114

she could feel her fingers. Then she said, "Well, I expect you do have a fracture, but we won't know for sure until we X-ray it. Come with me and we'll have you fixed up in no time." Dr. Morrison put an arm across Chloe's shoulders and escorted her gently out of the waiting area.

A couple of hours later Chloe's right arm was set in a cast. But it wasn't until she got home that she began to realize how difficult it was to do everything with her left hand. Just putting toothpaste on her toothbrush took enormous patience. *How am I ever going to clean stalls with one arm?* Chloe thought as she fumbled with the toothpaste.

Chloe finally managed to brush her teeth. She changed into a big, old T-shirt that had belonged to her father. Then she went to say good-night to her mother. At that moment the phone rang.

When Kathryn Goodman hung up, she wore a tired expression. "That was Mr. Sloane again," she said quietly.

Chloe stared at the floor and waited to hear what her mother would say. In her anxious state, she forgot all about her throbbing arm.

"He offered even more money for the pony," Ms. Goodman said. "Chloe, he offered twenty-five thousand dollars."

"Jump For Joy is not for sale," Chloe muttered, without looking up at her mother.

"Chloe, how are you ever going to take care of

that pony with a broken arm?" Ms. Goodman said. "How will you do your barn chores? You know we can't afford to pay the board on Jump For Joy, and Sharon's not going to let him stay there for free. You'll have to sell him. I just don't see any other way," Ms. Goodman pleaded.

Chloe didn't answer her mother. She went to her room and lay down on her bed. The fan whirred softly, stirring the eyelet curtains at the window. The blue light of the streetlight outside shone through the curtains and left a pattern of eyelet shadow upon Chloe's broken arm. She stared at the cast, wishing she could go back and undo the whole day. If only she had fed Jenny in the morning! Then the dog wouldn't have gotten into the food and scattered it. Chloe wouldn't have fallen and broken her arm. How was she going to clean stalls? How could she groom her pony or Bo Peep properly? She couldn't even tighten a girth, not with just one hand. And who would help her? She had thought she could count on Megan for anything, but after the last week, she wasn't so sure. Megan seemed more interested in be-friending Amanda Sloane so that she could ride Prince Charming. And Amanda was obviously inter-ested in just one thing: Jump For Joy.

Chloe knew that Amanda was used to having whatever she wanted. And she knew that Gerald Sloane was used to getting it for his daughter. Chloe was pretty sure that now that she had a broken arm, her mom would make her sell Jump For Joy back to the Sloanes. She wondered for a second if her dad would let her keep him—if she could somehow get to his house in Arkansas. She had been there once; he had a fenced-in backyard big enough for a pony. Would he let her live with him and keep Jump For Joy there?

All her life Chloe had dreamed of owning her own pony. She finally had him, the pony of her dreams. And suddenly it seemed as though all the forces of the universe had ganged up on her to keep her one dream from coming true. "Where are you?" she said aloud to the ceiling, thinking of the angel-fairy she often imagined. But she knew no winged spirit was going to suddenly heal her broken arm. She also knew that no mere person, least of all Amanda Sloane, was going to take away her pony, now that she had him.

Chloe decided that there was only one thing she could do to keep her pony. Lying awake in the lonely blue glow of the streetlight, she began to hatch a plan—a plan that she wouldn't tell to anyone, not even Megan. It was the only way she could be sure Jump For Joy wouldn't be taken from her, and she was determined to do it. Nobody and nothing would stop her.

The next day was Saturday. Chloe's mom took the day off to stay home with her daughter, though

Chloe did her best to convince her that she would be just fine without her. Chloe lay on the couch, pretending to read a book of animal hero stories. But what she was really doing was trying to figure out how to get to Thistle Ridge Farm.

"Phone's for you, Chloe," Ms. Goodman said, jarring Chloe out of her thoughts. "It's Megan."

"I don't feel like talking right now," Chloe said softly. She was afraid that Megan would tell her all about riding Prince Charming, or that Amanda had groomed Jump For Joy for her. Chloe's throat ached as she imagined her best friend having a sleep-over with Amanda Sloane. Why was everyone betraying her? What had she done to deserve it? Tears began to burn behind her eyes.

Ms. Goodman gave her a puzzled glance and relayed the message to Megan. When she hung up, she said to Chloe, "Megan says 'hey,' and she hopes your arm doesn't hurt. Is it hurting much, sweetie?" Ms. Goodman asked.

Chloe shook her head and brought the book closer to her face so that her mom wouldn't see that she was crying.

It took almost the whole day, but Chloe finally convinced her mother that she felt well enough to visit the barn. The sun had dropped close to the crest of the highest ridge beyond the farm as they turned up the long, tree-lined drive to Thistle Ridge. When they pulled up to the main barn,

Chloe grabbed her backpack and awkwardly opened the car door with her left hand.

"Oh, I forgot! I've got to pick up Michael at Mamaw's. It's her canasta night," Ms. Goodman said. "I'll be back to get you in about an hour."

"Okay, Mama." Chloe started to get out of the car.

"Chloe, what do you need that backpack for?" Ms. Goodman said. She was staring at her daughter's school backpack, which appeared to be stuffed full of something.

"Oh, it's just some grooming equipment and my boots," Chloe said quickly. "See you later!" she called, slamming the car door. She waved to her mom and made herself stand and wait until the orange Pinto had disappeared. Then she hurried into the barn.

The horses had already been given their evening grain. Chloe was relieved to see that no one was around. The grooms had gone home for the day, and the lessons were done, so no instructors were about. Red-golden sunlight slanted in the door at one end of the barn, making Chloe squint as she headed down the aisle toward Jump For Joy's stall. On the way, she noticed that Prince Charming's stall was empty. *I bet the Sloanes sold him already,* Chloe thought.

Jump For Joy raised his head at the sound of his mistress's voice and gave a little nicker of greeting.

Chloe smiled when she saw him, but her expression was tense as she went into the stall and tried to put his halter on him. She couldn't get it buckled with one arm, so she gave up and went and got the bridle. She knew she shouldn't tack up the pony in his stall, but she couldn't get him on cross-ties without the halter.

Fortunately, Jump For Joy was easy to bridle. Chloe hung the reins around his neck, then pulled the crownpiece up until the bit touched his lips. He opened his mouth and took the bit complacently, and Chloe slipped the crownpiece over his ears and adjusted the throatlatch.

The saddle was harder to put on. Chloe managed to lift it onto his back, and even got the girth tight by loosening it first on the off side so she could buckle it easily on the near. She went back to tighten the off side and last, the near. Then she realized his legs weren't wrapped.

"Oh, no," she said. "How'm I going to wrap his legs with one hand?" she wondered aloud. But when she tried, she found that she could gingerly use her broken arm to hold the top of the polo wrap until she had it started. It took less than five minutes to wrap both front legs, and it wasn't a bad job. *I used to do much worse with both hands*, she thought.

When she had the pony tacked up, Chloe slipped her backpack carefully over her broken arm, then

120

shouldered the other strap. It wasn't full of grooming equipment, as she had told her mother. Chloe had packed it with a jacket, a bottle of water, some peanut butter sandwiches, and her favorite book of animal stories. She peered out of the stall door. Not a groom was in sight. She quickly led Jump For Joy out the back door and down the wheelbarrow path to the old section of fence that hid the manure pile. No one would see her there. She pulled down the stirrups and mounted up, using the bottom rail of the old fence for a step. Jump For Joy swung his head around and gazed at her for a moment. His expression seemed to say, "Well, this is a little unusual, but as long as you know where you're going, I'm with you."

Chloe slid her hand up his silky neck and patted him. Then she gathered up the reins in her one good hand and walked boldly down the driveway under the pecan trees and past the white-fenced paddocks to the main road. At the bottom of the drive Chloe stopped, glancing up at the sign hanging from the cedar post, which read Thistle Ridge Farm. She thought of all the wonderful times she had had there, especially since she had found her good friends in the Short Stirrup Club. She would miss them, especially Megan. "But they won't miss me," she said to her pony. Then she turned left onto the road that led to the highway to Memphis, where she could cross the Mississippi river into Arkansas.

Jump For Joy walked obediently along the dusty shoulder of the road. Wildflowers grew there, some just beginning to close up their delicate cups in the cooler evening air. Sometimes a toad hopped away from the pony's feet as they clopped along. Chloe heard the lonely, three-note call of a whippoorwill before she saw it, sitting alone in the middle of the road. It called out to her again as she passed, then flew up into a tree. She heard it singing forlornly behind her as she rode on, reminding her that night was coming on. Chloe felt as lonely as that whippoorwill as she continued down the deserted road.

It was a couple of miles to where the county road junctioned with the highway to Memphis. Chloe hoped she could make it to the crossroads before dark. The highway was lit with bright sodium lamps, and she could easily ride along the wide shoulder all the way to Memphis. Before long the county road would be dark; she urged Jump For Joy into a quicker walk, noticing that lightning bugs were beginning to blink green in the heavy air.

The evening sky held the last glowing light of the long, hot day as she glimpsed the highway overpass. Chloe bent forward into two-point position as Jump For Joy stepped willingly up the embankment toward the highway. It was brighter on the highway. The sodium lights hummed loud and pink, each bright circle of light joining into the next. Chloe could walk all the way to Memphis through those linked circles of light. She felt proud and determined as Jump For Joy picked his way along the broad gravel shoulder of the road.

The county road had been quiet in comparison to the four-lane, which had much more traffic on it. Cars roared loudly by, their headlights glaring. Chloe could feel her pony's body tense and his steps quicken every time a car passed. They had not gone more than fifty yards when a huge truck came barreling down the highway. Just as it passed them, the driver honked at another car. The blast of the horn startled the pony, and his head shot up. He trotted quickly for a several strides before Chloe got him to walk again. She began to wonder if walking down the highway was such a good idea after all. "Don't worry, pony," Chloe said to reassure him, though she was really trying to reassure herself. "When we get to Dad's, everything will be just fine." But in her heart she wasn't so sure.

Just then another truck went by. It was a big horse transport van. It slowed down, then turned off at the exit ramp to the road Chloe had just come from. A pickup truck followed it. In a panicked instant, Chloe recognized the green-and-gold lettering on the side of the horse van. It was the van from Thistle Ridge Farm, returning from a horse show. And she was sure Jake had been following along in his blue pickup, as he always did, to see that everything was safe.

"Do you think they saw us?" Chloe said anxiously to Jump For Joy.

In another minute she had an answer to that question. When she looked over her shoulder, the blue pickup truck was turning onto the highway again. "Shoot!" Chloe exclaimed. "They did see us." She urged Jump For Joy into a trot, moving as far as she dared out of the light of the sodium lamps. "Maybe they won't notice us in the shadows," Chloe said. But when she glanced back again, the truck headlights were approaching.

Suddenly Chloe felt complete panic overwhelm her. She imagined Jake bringing her and her pony back to the barn. Everyone would say there was no way she could care for the pony properly. They would tell her she was reckless for taking him on the highway like that after he had just recovered from his torn suspensory ligament. Everyone would agree that Jump For Joy should go back to Amanda. They would insist it was just a fluke that Chloe had ended up with him in the first place.

In desperation, Chloe kicked at her pony's sides and felt him canter on. She knew it was dangerous. She couldn't see the footing in the shadows, and she had never cantered him before. But all Chloe could think was that no one was going to take her pony away. She bent into two-point, feeling his mane lash against her face. She kicked him again as hard as she could and heard his feet crunching through the gravel as he galloped down the highway. She shouted into his ears, "Go! Go! Go!" as sobs tore her throat and her broken arm throbbed in the same pounding rhythm of his gallop.

But suddenly the pony's pace dropped to a canter, then a trot, as his head swung back and forth. He slowed to a walk, his ears moving all around, as if he were listening for something. Then he came to a complete stop. Chloe kicked him again, but he refused to go any further. It was as if Jump For Joy had heard some other higher command he was determined to obey. No matter how Chloe tried, she couldn't get him to move on. "Pony! They'll catch us! Don't you understand?" she cried. "Please, please, go on, go on," she begged him. "They'll take you away. I'll lose you forever!" Chloe gave up at last and collapsed on the pony's neck, sobbing broken-heartedly.

She heard the crunch of the tires on the shoulder of the road as the truck pulled over and stopped behind her, its engine running. With dread she listened to feet approaching on the gravel, one heavy and one light.

"Is it her?" she heard Megan's voice say.

"Chloe, is that you?" Jake Wyndham called anxiously.

"Leave us alone. Just leave us alone!" Chloe shouted. She raised her head and tried once more to get her pony to move, but he just stood there patiently, as if he knew what was best. Chloe jumped off and started trying to lead the pony with her good arm.

"Chloe, stop!" Megan said, sounding alarmed. "Why are you doing this?"

"I'm running away, can't you tell?" Chloe yelled. "Only I can't even do that right! I can't do anything right! You'll all be better off without me. But nobody is taking my pony away, do you hear? *Nobody!*" Chloe began sobbing all over again. She stumbled as she tried to lead Jump For Joy down the road.

"What's she talkin' about?" Jake asked, bewildered. "Who's tryin' to take her pony away?"

"The Sloanes!" Chloe shouted. "They want him back for Amanda because she's too scared to get on Prince Charming. They tried to buy him back. They offered my mother a lot of money, and I know she'll make me do it; she'll make me sell him! Just because they want Amanda to win some stupid big horse show. Well, they can't have him. I'm taking him away to live with my father, and don't you try to stop me!"

"Chloe, the Sloanes don't want him back. I mean,

they probably did, but they don't anymore," Megan said. "It's okay. You won't have to worry about it."

"That's what you said before," Chloe said. "And then they tried to buy him. And you knew it all along. You didn't care. You just wanted to ride Prince Charming. You're not my friend!" Chloe said, and her heart ached even more than her arm when she thought how Megan had betrayed her.

"Chloe, you've got it all wrong!" Megan protested. "That's not how it is at all! I was riding Prince Charming to school him for Amanda. And I was just hanging around with her so I could convince her to get back on him, so she'd stop bugging her parents to buy Jump For Joy. And it worked! I schooled Prince Charming all week. Today Amanda rode Prince Charming in the Charity Classic Horse Show and she won the Short Stirrup division. Chloe, the Sloanes are happy with Prince Charming now. They won't be interested in Jump For Joy."

Chloe turned around in disbelief. "Is that really true?" she asked.

"It is," Jake told her. "Amanda did right well on that rotten ol' horse of hers. He took her around like an angel."

"I'm sorry that you thought I wasn't being your friend," Megan added softly. Chloe heard Megan's voice waver as she spoke. "Please don't be mad at me. I was just trying to help."

Suddenly an orange Pinto pulled off the highway

127

right behind Jake's truck. Chloe's mom got out, followed by Max, Keith, and Sharon.

"Chloe!" Kathryn Goodman cried in relief. "Thank goodness we found you." She rushed to hug her daughter.

"Are you okay, Chloe?" Sharon said worriedly. "When Megan spotted you by the road out here, at first I didn't believe her. Then Jake pulled us over and told me he thought he'd seen you, too. What in the world are you doing out here all alone on the highway?"

Chloe's throat was still choked with emotion. She was glad the Sloanes wouldn't be trying to get Jump For Joy anymore, but she still didn't know how she was going to clean stalls with a broken arm. "Sharon, I broke my arm," she managed to blurt out.

"Yes, I heard," Sharon replied. "I hope it's better soon."

"I don't know how I'll be able to clean stalls and do my barn chores to work off Jump For Joy's board," Chloe said.

"We'll all help you, won't we guys?" Megan said to Max and Keith.

"Of course," Keith said.

"Short Stirrup Club to the rescue!" Max sang out.

"You will?" Chloe said skeptically.

"Sure," Max said. "I sort of like cleaning stalls."

"Me, too," Megan agreed.

"I don't," Keith said, wrinkling his nose. "But I'll do it anyway," he said with a grin.

"Oh, I'm such a dope," Chloe said, smiling through her tears. "I thought nobody cared about me, but boy, was I wrong. I'm sorry I doubted you, Megan," she said.

Megan gave her best friend an affectionate squeeze.

"I don't need a guardian angel," Chloe said. "I have the Short Stirrup Club. And Jump For Joy knew it all the time. I guess that's why he wouldn't go on anymore, even when I tried to make him."

Jump For Joy chose that moment to nod his head, for all the world as if he were agreeing with her. They all laughed, and Chloe patted her pony. Somewhere nearby, a whippoorwill called again, but for some reason his call didn't sound lonely to Chloe anymore. He sounded as glad as Chloe felt, surrounded by people who cared, and a pony of her very own.

About the Author

ALLISON ESTES grew up in Oxford, Mississippi. She wrote, bound, and illustrated her first book when she was five years old, learned to drive her grandfather's truck when she was eight, and got her first pony when she was ten. She has been writing, driving trucks, and riding horses ever since.

Allison is a trainer at Claremont Riding Academy, the only riding stable in New York City. She currently lives in Manhattan with her seven-year-old daughter, Megan, who spends every spare moment around, under, or on horses.